WILD VET ADVENTURES

SAVING ANIMALS AROUND THE WORLD
With Dr. Gabby Wild

GABBY WILD
With
JENNIFER SZYMANSKI

TABLE OF CONTENTS

NORTH
AMERICA
p. 150

SOUTH &
CENTRAL
AMERICA
p. 10

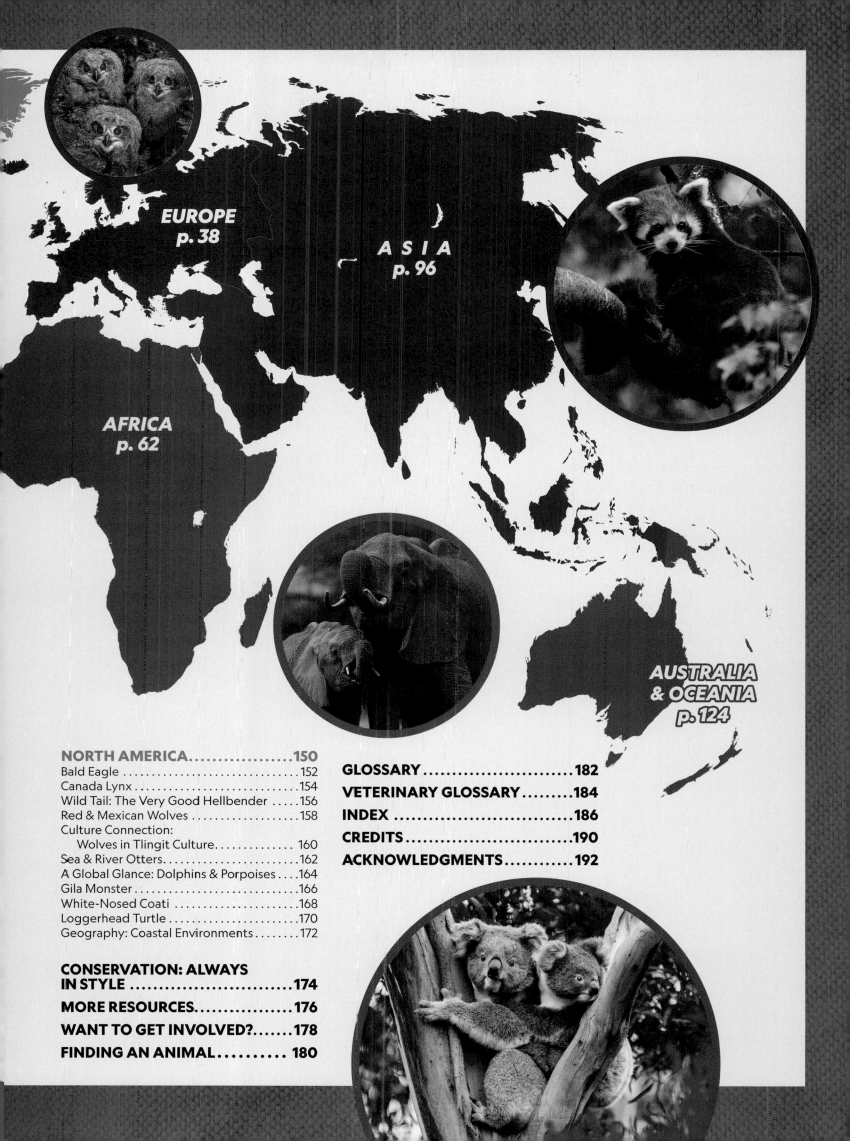

EUROPE
p. 38

ASIA
p. 96

AFRICA
p. 62

AUSTRALIA
& OCEANIA
p. 124

A WORD FROM GABBY

When I was a little girl, **ALL I WANTED TO DO WAS READ ABOUT WILD ANIMALS.** Every day I would study facts about different critters and dream of working with them. I was fascinated with science and animal medicine, too, and soon it became obvious that I should become a veterinarian. But not just any veterinarian—**I WANTED TO BECOME A WILDLIFE VETERINARIAN.** The life of a wild animal doctor is exciting, fun, and rewarding. No two days are ever the same because I get to work with so many different types of animals, and each species is so different and fascinating!

You do not need to be a wildlife veterinarian to love and protect animals, though. **EVERY PERSON CAN HELP ANIMALS** by working hard to keep the planet clean through simple acts like recycling, not littering, and making less unnecessary trash. We live on this planet together: people and animals. And **TOGETHER WE MUST RESPECT AND PROTECT IT.** After reading this book about some of my wild friends, I hope you will feel inspired to protect them and their homes, too. **AND MAYBE YOU'LL EVEN BECOME A WILDLIFE VETERINARIAN ONE DAY!**

How to Explore This Book:

This book will take you on a journey around the world. We'll visit six of Earth's seven continents, and learn about some of the kinds of wildlife you'll find on each. The animals don't live separated by the lines that make up a country or a city or a forest, though. They coexist in their ecosystems, and ours, unaware of human-made boundaries.

In each chapter, **YOU'LL MEET SOME OF MY FAVORITE PATIENTS.**

Check out the **EXAM TIME** section to learn more about some of the body parts that make each animal so unique.

LOOK FOR THE FOLLOWING SYMBOLS TO LEARN MORE ABOUT ...

- ♥ where each animal lives and what their family life is like
- 🍴 what they eat
- ⚡ the dangers they face, both from predators in the wild and those caused by people

Along the way, you'll **LEARN ABOUT SOME OF THE GEOGRAPHICAL FEATURES ON EACH CONTINENT** that are important to the animals that live there, as well as an example of a **SPECIAL RELATIONSHIP THAT EXISTS BETWEEN WILDLIFE AND PEOPLE.** On **GLOBAL GLANCE** pages, you'll even get to learn about a special challenge that a particular group of animals faces—as well as a little about what we're doing to take on that challenge.

Let's get started on our adventure!

STAY WILD,

Dr. Gabby Wild

A DAY IN THE LIFE OF A VET

What does a typical day in the life of a veterinarian look like? The answer is that there's hardly ever a typical day! Every exam of every animal can bring new questions to answer and new challenges to tackle.

We all know that animals can't talk to let us know that they're not feeling well. So you really have to be a sort of detective to be a good veterinarian. The results of an examination give me clues to what might be wrong. The first part of my job is to put these clues together to try to figure out what's going on. Once I know the problem, I can figure out how to make the animal feel better!

There are a few questions I ask even before every exam, whether it's in the wild, in a zoo, or at my clinic. They include:

"Who's here?" The basic answer to this question is called the signalment. It includes the animal's species, age, and whether it's male or female.

"Why are they here?" Why did the animal come in today? Is it for a checkup? Does it have the sniffles? Something else?

"What's been going on?" I take a good look at what we call the animal's history. If it's a pet, does it have all its shots? Has it been sick recently? The more clues I have, the more likely it is that I can put the puzzle together.

These steps might go something like this:

Who's here?

 5-year, 10-month-old female Labrador retriever

 3-month-old male snow leopard

Why is the patient here?

 She's been limping for two days on the left back leg and cries when she puts weight on it.

 He has a runny nose, is sleeping more than usual, and seems to have some difficulty breathing.

What's been going on?

 She went on a hike with her owner two days ago and has come to see me before with a sore knee.

 He was orphaned in the wild, rescued, and brought to my clinic.

After I find out the animal's history, it's time to meet the patient!

What happens in an animal visit is a lot like what happens in your doctor visits.

- I find out how much the animal weighs.
- I listen to its heart and breathing.
- I feel its belly and other parts of its body.

Younger animals and older animals get a bit of special treatment at an exam. I look at baby or young animals to make sure they are growing properly and are gaining enough weight.

I look at an older animal's teeth to make sure they are healthy. Unhealthy teeth might mean the animal isn't able to chew its food well. If that's the case, the animal might not be getting enough nutrition from its food. Older animals also have more bone and joint problems than younger animals.

WHAT'S THAT SHOT?

Animals get vaccines (shots) to keep them from getting certain kinds of diseases. Here are just a few of the common vaccines that animals get.

NAME OF THE VACCINE	WHAT DOES IT DO?
Rabies	The rabies shot protects your pet from getting rabies. This disease is caused by a very tiny germ called a virus that affects the brain. All mammals (including people) can get rabies, but we usually see it in wild animals like skunks, foxes, and raccoons, which can carry the disease.
Distemper	The distemper shot in dogs and cats helps keep your pet from getting a few different diseases. These diseases affect body parts like the lungs, nose and throat, and stomach. People cannot catch distemper.
Lyme Disease	Lyme disease can cause fever and a rash. It is often spread by ticks, which can bite people and pets when they are outside.

One other thing I always think about when I'm examining an animal is keeping myself safe—it's no fun getting bitten or scratched by even the smallest puppy.

Most pets that come to the clinic can be held and kept calm by either their owners or by one of my helpers.

Even though animals at the zoo are still wild animals, they're much more used to people than animals that live, say, in the rainforest. Zoo animals can be trained (at least a little!) to learn what to expect during a vet exam. For example, a big cat can be trained to put its paws up to the fence of its enclosure. Then I can have a good look at them—and the cat gets a treat for helping me out!

If I need to take a close look at an animal at a zoo, I give the animal anesthesia with a bit of a special gas or sometimes a shot. The anesthesia puts the animal to sleep for a little bit. Since wild animals aren't trained, I also always use anesthesia in the wild, no matter what I'm examining—this is safest for me, my team, and the animal.

SOUTH & CENTRAL AMERICA

Central and South America cover **AN ENORMOUS AREA,** ranging from the northern border of Belize to Chile's Cape Horn. In between, you'll find **DESERTS, RAINFORESTS, MOUNTAINS, GRASSLANDS,** and even **GLACIERS!** It's no surprise, then, that these two regions of the world are home to an incredible number of wildlife species.

After working with jaguars in Central America, I fell in love with the **UNIQUE WILDLIFE** of this area, like the tapir pictured above. I try to find every opportunity I can to work with injured wildlife there. I also love to treat local farmers' livestock, especially their alpacas and llamas!

CLAIMS TO FAME

More than **3,000** kinds of fish

The world's LARGEST snake: the giant anaconda (weighing up to 550 pounds [250 kg])

More than **1,300** kinds of birds

2.5 million kinds of insects in the Amazon rainforest alone!

The world's LARGEST rodent: the capybara (weighing up to 150 pounds [68 kg])

SOUTH AMERICAN
PENGUINS

✚ Meet the Patient

The word "penguin" probably brings to mind the cold, ice, and snow. But not all penguins live in the frigid Antarctic! Some like it a bit warmer. Seven species of penguins make their homes off the coasts of South America.

♥ Habitat and Family

South American penguins live on islands and coasts near the ocean. Penguins nest in large groups called colonies. These groups can be huge, with thousands of birds at breeding time. A pair of penguins works together to raise their chicks.

🍽 Diet

Penguins are carnivorous birds, and eat fish, squid, shrimp, and other sea animals. They can also drink the salty ocean water they swallow as they gulp down their prey. Penguins have a special body part above each eye that helps them get rid of the extra salt so they don't get sick.

⚡ Dangers

PREDATORS: some kinds of seals and sharks, and carnivorous whales

HUMAN CONFLICT: climate change, overfishing, habitat loss

🔍 Exam Time

Penguin flippers aren't exactly like dolphins' and whales' flippers. They're extremely sleek wings, and they help these birds speed through the water, sometimes as fast as 30 miles an hour (48 km/h)!

Most birds have some bones that are hollow. Hollow bones are lighter, which helps flight. Penguins, on the other hand, have dense, heavy bones. This allows them to swim below the surface instead of floating to the top of the water.

Like all adult birds, penguins do not have teeth. Penguins have a hooked tongue that helps them to grab on to slippery fish during a meal.

Penguins have special clear eyelids to help them hunt underwater. They act like goggles, protecting their eyes while helping them see clearly.

GALÁPAGOS PENGUIN

MAGELLANIC PENGUIN

GABBY SAYS!

One of the most common problems with giving anesthesia to an animal is that the animal often gets really cold after receiving it. But that's not the case with penguins! These birds have waterproof feathers that keep them super warm, and the special way that blood flows through their legs and wings helps keep their bodies warm during chilly ocean swims. So if I have to give a penguin anesthesia, I put ice packs on their limbs instead of a blanket, so they don't overheat!

GALÁPAGOS TORTOISE

✚ Meet the Patient

This gentle reptile is the world's largest kind of tortoise. It's also one of the longest living animals on Earth. Most Galápagos tortoises live to be well over 100 years old, and some animals have been known to live to 170!

♥ Habitat and Family

The climate on each of the Galápagos Islands is a little bit different, so these tortoises are adapted to live in both dry, rocky areas and wetter, greener areas. It just depends on the island! Tortoises don't hang out in groups. They are quite territorial and will fight off another tortoise that tries to move in. When it's time to lay eggs, female tortoises find a warm spot and dig a hole. They mix some dirt together with pee and cover the eggs, leaving them to hatch.

🍽 Diet

The Galápagos tortoise is a herbivore, feeding on grasses and fruits such as cactus pears. Young tortoises eat about 17 percent of their body weight every day!

⚡ Dangers

PREDATORS: hawks, domestic animals
HUMAN CONFLICT: poaching, loss of habitat to development of land for farms and homes

🔍 Exam Time

SPACED-OUT SHELL: This tortoise's shell, or carapace (CARE-uh-pace), has spaces on the inside that make it look like a honeycomb. These spaces make the shell light. If it were solid, it would be too heavy for the tortoise to move.

STRETCHABLE NECK: Many Galápagos tortoises have a long neck that they use to reach for plants to eat. They also sometimes use their neck in a competition: Whichever animal stretches its neck higher wins!

TWO BLADDERS: When a Galápagos tortoise has a drink, it makes that drink count! These reptiles have two bladders they can use to store water for up to a year.

ALL-TERRAIN LEGS: The rocky Galápagos Islands can make for some rough ground. So the Galápagos tortoise has thick and sturdy legs to help it move over the uneven landscape. Its walk is also sort of a waddle: Its front legs push up its body, then its back legs scoot the tortoise forward.

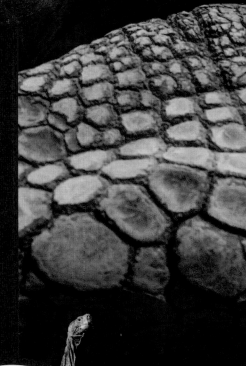

GABBY SAYS!

Turtle and tortoise shells are made of a material that feels like bone. Whenever we find a tortoise with a cracked or broken shell, we have to treat it like a broken bone! This means we must make sure that the shell is getting all the nutrients it needs to heal, and we are very careful to watch for infection.

GALÁPAGOS ISLANDS
ECUADOR

The Galápagos Islands are found off the western coast of Ecuador. This group of islands, sometimes called an archipelago (ark-ih-PELL-ih-go), was formed by underwater volcanoes. Although there are more than a hundred islands in the chain, only a few of them have people living on them. That makes the Galápagos a great place for studying and watching wildlife.

SALLY LIGHTFOOT CRABS HAVE AN IMPORTANT JOB: THEY SCAVENGE MANY KINDS OF FOOD, WHICH HELPS KEEP THEIR ENVIRONMENT CLEAN.

LAND IGUANAS GET MOST OF THE WATER THEY NEED FROM EATING THE CACTI THAT GROW ON THE ISLANDS

 Fast Facts

» The underwater life found around some of the islands has made the Galápagos one of the "Seven Underwater Wonders of the World." Large groups of sea turtles, hammerhead sharks, manta rays, and many other sea creatures are regularly seen by visitors and scientists.

» When Spanish sailors first came to the islands, they encountered some of the many tortoises that make their home here. These tortoises also helped the islands earn their name: An old Spanish word for "tortoise" is *galápago*.

» Some of the animals on the Galápagos are found nowhere else on Earth.

Plant Life

Although Ecuador is full of tropical plants, the Galápagos Islands are mostly rather dry (except for the tops of mountains), with desert-like plants covering the land. Expect to see plenty of cacti if you visit.

★ Good News

The Galápagos are very special, and because of that, people are only allowed to live in certain areas, which amount to 100 square miles (260 sq km) total. The rest of the islands are protected as a national park.

CHARLES DARWIN was a scientist and world traveler, and someone who was absolutely fascinated by wildlife. He was especially interested in why there are so many different kinds of living things on Earth.

On a trip to the Galápagos, Darwin noticed that the tortoises living on islands with a lot of tall plants have longer necks that can stretch and reach these plants. On the islands with low-growing plants, the tortoises have shorter necks that cannot reach very high.

Darwin concluded that if a tortoise with a long neck is born on an island with tall plants, it would have an easier time getting food than a tortoise with a shorter neck would. The long-necked tortoise would be healthier and be able to have more long-necked babies. Eventually, all of the tortoises on that island would have long necks.

WILD FACT!

Capybaras have a habit of eating their own poop. They do this to replenish the bacteria that live inside their gut, which help digest the plants the capybaras eat.

GABBY SAYS!

Capybaras need a special diet that includes a lot of fresh leaves and fruits and vegetables. These foods help provide enough vitamin C. Just like people, capybaras need vitamin C to keep their gums, skin, and hair healthy.

CAPYBARA

✚ Meet the Patient

The world's largest rodent, the capybara, is related to guinea pigs, mice, and rats. Found mostly in eastern South America, capybaras can weigh up to 143 pounds (65 kg)! Capybaras can be pretty easygoing and tend to get along with many other animals.

♥ Habitat and Family

Capybaras have to keep their skin damp, so they live around marshes, ponds, and swamps.

Capybaras are social, living in herds of about 10 animals with one alpha male, or leader. However, when the weather is dry, they've been spotted hanging around water in groups of more than 40.

 Diet

During the wet seasons, capybaras eat reeds and fruits such as melons and squashes. When it's dry, they eat grass—up to eight pounds (3.6 kg) a day.

⚡ Dangers

PREDATORS: big cats, including jaguars; birds of prey; and reptiles such as anacondas and crocodiles

HUMAN CONFLICT: hunting, poaching for meat and hide

🔍 Exam Time

FABULOUS FAT: Capybaras have lots of fat under their skin. Not only does it keep them warm, it also helps them to float. This means they don't have to use as much energy to swim as some other kinds of animals.

ELEVATED EYES AND EARS: A capybara's eyes and small ears are way up on the top of the animal's head. This positioning helps it see and hear even when almost completely underwater.

THIN FUR: Capybaras' thin fur helps them stay cool in the heat, but it doesn't protect them from sunburn very well. When capybaras aren't swimming, they protect their skin by rubbing themselves in mud.

NOSE BUMP: A capybara has a bump on its nose called a morillo. It marks its territory by rubbing its morillo on trees and logs—similar to how cats rub against things in their surroundings to mark their territories.

TAPIR

✚ Meet the Patient

Is it a pig? An anteater? A hippo? Nope! These unique-looking animals are called tapirs and are most closely related to the rhino and the horse. Four of the world's five species of tapir are found in either South or Central America.

♥ Habitat and Family

Tapirs live in lowland forests, mountain forests, marshy areas, grasslands, and rainforests—anywhere it is reasonably damp. They are mostly solitary but occasionally travel in groups. Mother tapirs, called cows, raise their calves until they are about six months old. Calves are spotted and striped when they are small to help them blend into the leaves and brush.

🍽 Diet

Tapirs are herbivores, feeding on brush and leaves. Some also eat fruit. Tapirs eat a lot, up to about a quarter of their own body weight every day. Because they must eat so much, they spend most of the day searching for food.

⚡ Dangers

PREDATORS: crocodiles, big cats such as leopards and jaguars, large snakes

HUMAN CONFLICT: loss of habitat, poaching for meat and hide

🔍 Exam Time

PREHENSILE SNOUT: A tapir's nose and upper lip form a prehensile snout. The snout has muscles, just like an elephant's trunk! That means a tapir can wiggle its snout and use it to grab and pull on branches, stripping off the tender leaves to eat.

ROUNDED BODY: Tapirs have a solid, rounded body, with short legs and a stubby tail. This body shape helps a tapir crash through the thick brush and plant life of the forests where it lives.

FAIRLY FLAT FEET: Tapir toes are wide and spread out to help them walk on muddy banks. The shape of their feet also helps them keep their balance running up and down hills.

BRISTLY MANE: Most species of tapir have a row of thick bristles that helps protect their necks from jaguars and other predators.

WILD FACT!

Tapirs hang around the water for more than one reason. In addition to cooling off in it, tapirs need water to poop. The tapir you see in the water at the zoo might be using the restroom!

GABBY SAYS!

Tapirs love a good back scratch. I'll sometimes make sure zoo tapirs get a back scratch during an exam because it can keep them from wandering off! This trick only works if they are used to people, though—it's not something I'd try on a wild tapir.

GABBY SAYS!

Because howler monkeys spend most of their time in trees, the most common way to catch one if it's sick or needs a physical examination is to anesthetize it with a small dart; then we can climb up to bring it down. I always make sure there's lots of padding under the monkey we're targeting, just in case the monkey falls out of the tree. I definitely don't want the animal to get hurt!

HOWLER MONKEY

✚ Meet the Patient

About 100 species of monkeys live in South and Central America. Howler monkeys are one of the biggest—and they're definitely the noisiest! Howler monkeys greet the morning with loud calls that can be heard more than three miles (4.8 km) away.

♥ Habitat and Family

Howlers will spend their entire life in the top of rainforest trees, never coming to the ground. Most kinds of howler monkeys live in troops of about 10 to 20. Each troop includes a few males and many females.

🍽 Diet

Howler monkeys are omnivores, and will eat both plants and meat. Their favorite food is fruit such as figs, nuts, and seeds, but they will eat flowers and leaves and raid birds' nests for eggs if they can find them.

⚡ Dangers

PREDATORS: large birds of prey
HUMAN CONFLICT: hunting, habitat loss, pet trade (taken and sold as pets)

🔍 Exam Time

The throat of the male howler monkey looks swollen from the outside, sort of like the way a person's throat is a bit larger around what we call the Adam's apple. These monkeys have an extra-large voice box that helps them make very loud sounds.

Howler monkeys have prehensile tails. That means they're able to use their tails to hang on to a tree or branch, just as you would use your arms and hands. Prehensile tails allow howler monkeys to hang from a tree branch while still having their hands free.

Howler monkeys have a really good sense of smell, which helps them find food. They can smell fruits and nuts up to about two miles (3.2 km) away.

AMPHIBIANS

Amphibians belong to a group of animals that includes toads, frogs, and salamanders. They're found in places where there is plenty of freshwater, on every continent except for Antarctica.

HOUSTON TOAD, TEXAS, NORTH AMERICA

Although toads can spend a lot of time on land, they need to live in damp areas to keep their skin moist. Because of drought, the number of Houston toads has plummeted. Recently, more than a million zoo-bred toad eggs were placed in the wild, with the hope that the population will recover.

NORTH AMERICA

BROOK NEWT, CATALAN, SPAIN

Brook newts are different from most amphibians in that they spend their entire life in water. They're hard to find, and when one is caught, it releases a sticky, smelly slime that makes you want to drop it back into the water!

GLASS FROG, CENTRAL AND SOUTH AMERICA

Glass frogs live in the humid rainforests of South and Central America. They live their entire life in the trees, dropping down only to lay eggs in flowing water.

SOUTH AMERICA

⚡ Dangers

Although most amphibians live on land much of their life, they lay their eggs—and their offspring grow—in pools of water such as ponds and puddles. Climate change can decrease the amount of rain in an area, which can mean fewer pools or shallow streams and rivers. Climate change also causes temperatures in an area to vary, making it difficult for amphibians to know when to lay their eggs.

COLD-BLOODED

ᒌ Health

Amphibians all over the world can get a disease caused by a chytrid (KY-trid) fungus. A factor thought to contribute to the spread of this disease is higher temperatures caused by global climate change. As a vet, I make sure to check for and treat the chytrid disease whenever possible. I also test the water where amphibians might live to make sure it is free from disease and pollution.

Because amphibians spend parts of their life in the water and parts on land, they are often considered indicator species. How well an amphibian species is doing tells us a lot about the land and the water. If an indicator amphibian species isn't doing too well, that is an important problem. And once we know there's a problem, we can start figuring out a solution.

WHERE THESE AMPHIBIANS LIVE

■ Brook Newt
■ Chinese Giant Salamander
■ Glass Frog
■ Houston Toad
■ Western Leopard Toad
■ Yellow-Spotted Tree Frog

EUROPE

ASIA

AFRICA

CHINESE GIANT SALAMANDER, CENTRAL, SOUTH-WESTERN, AND SOUTHERN CHINA

This amphibian is truly a giant, as it can grow to be almost six feet (2 m) long! Giant salamanders like cool mountain streams and lakes and don't thrive if water temperatures get too warm (above 68°F, or 20°C).

YELLOW-SPOTTED TREE FROG, SOUTHEASTERN AUSTRALIA

Yellow-spotted tree frogs lay their eggs in the dense plants that grow in swamps and ponds. Once thought to be extinct because of the chytrid disease, a small group of frogs was recently spotted, and people are working together to increase their numbers.

AUSTRALIA & OCEANIA

WESTERN LEOPARD TOAD, SOUTH AFRICA

These colorful spotted toads are found only on Africa's South Cape. They make their way to shallow pools to breed on warm, rainy nights in spring.

25

TARANTULA

⊕ Meet the Patient

As a wildlife vet, I can't exclude any creatures from my care—even giant hairy spiders! These spiders might be scary-looking, but they're generally quite shy and gentle.

♥ Habitat and Family

Spiders, as a rule, are solitary, and tarantulas are no exception. They live in underground burrows. After mating, the female makes a silk cocoon in her burrow. She lays between 75 to 1,000 eggs, seals the cocoon, and guards the eggs until they hatch.

Diet

Tarantulas are carnivores. Most kinds eat insects, but bigger species eat toads and frogs, as well as small mammals like mice.

Dangers

PREDATORS: birds, amphibians, reptiles

HUMAN CONFLICT: poaching, habitat loss, people who kill them out of fear

⌕ Exam Time

Spiders aren't the same as insects—they belong to a separate group called arachnids. Insects have three body parts. Arachnids have only two: an abdomen and the cephalothorax, which includes the head and middle.

Despite having more than one pair of eyes, tarantulas see very poorly. They can't see color at all! They find prey by sensing air movement with the hair that covers their bodies.

Spiders can climb just about anywhere, even upside down! They're able to cling to smooth surfaces because the ends of their legs are covered with tiny hairs that can slip into the smallest cracks on a rock or tree.

Tarantulas don't generally bite unless they need to. Instead, they keep predators away by using their legs to flick special hairs from their abdomens. If a predator gets one of these hairs in its eye, it will likely leave the spider alone.

MEXICAN FIRELEG TARANTULA

WILD FACT! Tarantulas use their venom to catch prey like crickets and other small animals. It takes a lot of venom to kill a big bug!

GABBY SAYS!

Do vets really treat spiders? Absolutely! If a spider injures a leg, sometimes the best thing I can do as a vet is to carefully remove it. Once the old leg is safely off, the tarantula can grow a new one. Tarantulas also can get infections around their fangs, so I check to make sure they are clean.

GABBY SAYS!

Ever been licked by a cat and actually had it hurt? Once, I was nursing back to health a jaguar that needed some grooming. A jaguar's tongue feels very rough, like a cat's tongue. The tongue is covered with tiny little bumps called papillae (puh-PILL-ee) that help lick meat off bones and clean themselves of loose fur and dirt.

JAGUAR

➕ Meet the Patient

Jaguars are the biggest cat in the Americas, and the third largest in the world. Jaguars can be found throughout South and Central America but can be hard to spot because the number of these animals in the wild is steadily decreasing.

♥ Habitat and Family

Jaguars tend to live in forests, but are occasionally found in desert areas. Jaguars live alone, and will aggressively defend their territory, which they mark with scratches on trees or by scent. Female jaguars have one to four cubs in a litter, and raise them until the cubs are about two years old.

🍽 Diet

Jaguars are carnivores, and prey on at least 85 different types of animals, including tapirs, deer, turtles, and crocodiles.

⚡ Dangers

PREDATORS: smaller jaguars: anaconda

HUMAN CONFLICT: hunting and poaching for fur, habitat loss

🔍 Exam Time

In addition to using its tail for balance, a jaguar uses it as a fishing lure: It dips its tail into the water, twitching it to attract fish.

A jaguar has one of the strongest bites of any big cat: 1,350 pounds per square inch (95 kg/sq cm). With this incredible force, it can bite through extremely tough material, even turtle shells!

A jaguar's fur color depends on where it lives. Jaguars that live in shady forests usually have darker coats than those that live in open areas.

WILD TAIL!

MY SCARIEST STORY

Many people ask me about my scariest experiences. There's no doubt that my vet visit in Belize with a jaguar named Pirate ranks the highest!

One of the things I see in big cats that live in zoos is tooth and gum decay. Sometimes they don't get enough of the nutrients they need to keep their mouths healthy. Pirate, who lived at a zoo in Belize, Central America, had been having some difficulty with his teeth, and he needed a root canal—something that people see a dentist for; for animals, it's done by their regular vet.

In order to do Pirate's dental work, we had to give him anesthesia. The gas we used comes from a machine that needs electricity to run. I was halfway through the dental work when a big storm came up. One flash of lightning, and out went the power! Fortunately, the hospital has backup ways to get power. Not just one, but two, generators were at the ready.

The storm went on, as did my work. Suddenly, the first generator stopped working. I still wasn't losing my cool, even though I had my fingers in the jaguar's mouth. After all, there was a second backup generator. We weren't happy, but every-thing was still good, and I only needed 15 more minutes to finish. I was almost done.

Then ... the second generator stopped. What luck—and me with my hand in this cat's mouth! I looked at my team, knowing that I had less than two minutes before all of the anesthesia would wear off, and I would be working in the mouth of a very big, very crabby, very AWAKE jaguar!

I finished as quickly as I could, and making sure that Pirate was okay, hurried to help get him back to his enclosure. I didn't even take him off the stretcher—I just got out. I was barely out and the zookeeper had just locked the door, when Pirate jumped to his feet. I had barely escaped a BIG bite!

ANIMALS—EVEN BIG PREDATORS LIKE JAGUARS—CAN GET TOOTH DECAY, JUST LIKE HUMANS. PIRATE NEEDED A ROOT CANAL TO SAVE ONE OF HIS TEETH.

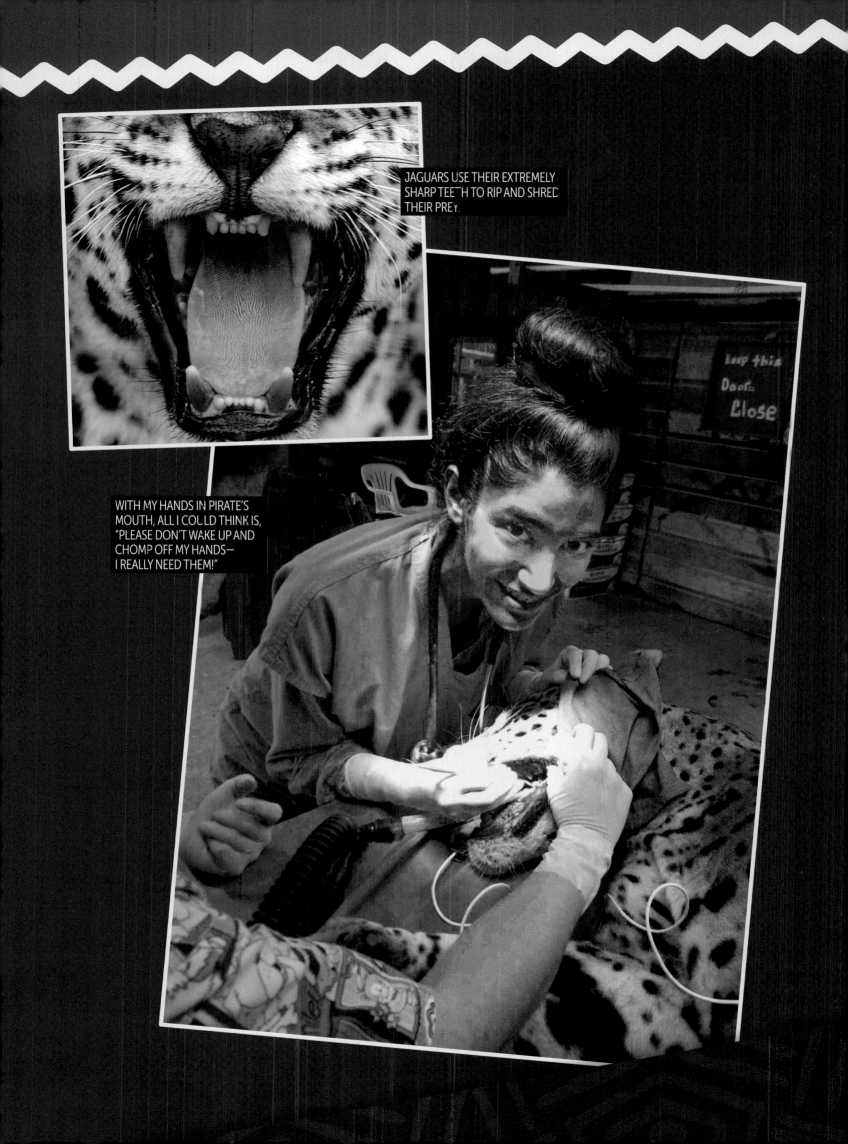

JAGUARS USE THEIR EXTREMELY SHARP TEETH TO RIP AND SHRED THEIR PREY.

WITH MY HANDS IN PIRATE'S MOUTH, ALL I COULD THINK IS, "PLEASE DON'T WAKE UP AND CHOMP OFF MY HANDS—I REALLY NEED THEM!"

KINKAJOU

⊕ Meet the Patient

Kinkajous can be found prowling the forests of South and Central America at night, searching for food. Although its long tail and big eyes make the kinkajou look a bit like a monkey, it's not a primate—this animal is most closely related to the raccoon.

♥ Habitat and Family

Kinkajous live almost their entire life in trees, rarely coming down to the ground. They don't live in groups but will come together to groom each other and to play. Mother kinkajous have one baby at a time. The baby grows quickly and can hang by its tail at about two months of age, but its mother tends to it until it's a little over a year old.

🍽 Diet

Kinkajous are grouped with other carnivores because of their sharp teeth. However, kinkajous eat mostly fruit and flower nectar. Occasionally they will eat insects, eggs, or small mammals.

⚡ Dangers

PREDATORS: ocelots, jaguars, eagles

HUMAN CONFLICT: habitat loss

🔍 Exam Time

SMALL BUT POWERFUL EARS Although the kinkajou's ears are small, its hearing is sensitive enough to hear a snake slithering through the trees.

WARM, WOOLLY COAT The kinkajou's fur is very thick. The hairs are so tightly packed together that water from a rain shower runs right off the animal's back, keeping it dry.

ROPELIKE TAIL Like monkeys, a kinkajou can use its tail to grab on to branches in its leafy home. It can also use its tail as a rope—it will climb up its own tail to return to the branch it's hanging from.

LONG, SLENDER TONGUE A kinkajou's tongue is about five inches (13 cm) long! This long tongue helps it reach the sweet nectar in the bottom of flowers.

AMAZING ANKLES Kinkajous can run up or down a tree quickly because they are able to turn their ankles around and run down a tree trunk headfirst.

GABBY SAYS!

When I walked up to my first kinkajou, I nearly fell over from fear. There, right in front of me, was the cutest little critter ... making the scariest of shrieking sounds! Some say they sound like a person screaming, and one native group supposedly named them *la llorona* ("the crier") for that reason. In fact, some of my colleagues even use earplugs when working with them.

VICUÑA &
GUANACO

✚ Meet the Patient

Don't be surprised if these animals look familiar—they're the wild cousins of llamas and alpacas. Vicuñas (vick-COON-yaz) and guanacos (gwa-NAH-koz) roam the South American countries of Peru, Argentina, Bolivia, and Chile.

GUANACOS

❤ Habitat and Family

Vicuñas and guanacos live in herds of about 15 animals on South American mountains and plains. One male leads each herd—other males may hang out in bachelor groups until they start herds of their own. Mothers give birth to one baby, called a calf, each year. The baby will stay with its mother for about a year.

🍽 Diet

Vicuñas and guanacos are herbivores and eat grasses, shrubs, and other tough, chewy plants.

⚡ Dangers

PREDATORS: mountain lions, foxes

HUMAN CONFLICT: habitat loss

🔍 Exam Time

SPLIT UPPER LIP An upper lip that is split in two helps the guanaco and vicuña grab and pull up plants, and even very short grasses.

TOUGH TUMMY Life on the dry plains and in the mountains can mean a diet of some pretty tough plants. These animals can handle it, though—they have a special stomach that has three parts, a little bit like a cow's stomach.

SQUISHY HOOVES Guanacos and vicuñas have hooves. They're much softer than deer or horse hooves, and are split into two toes. This shape helps the animals climb the rough, rocky ground of their home.

GUANACO

VICUÑA

GABBY SAYS!

"For the most part, vicuñas and guanacos tend to be pretty relaxed in the company of humans. Their calm nature made them excellent animals for people to domesticate, or make tame. Eventually, the domesticated vicuñas and guanacos became the llamas and alpacas found today on farms all over the world."

A LONG LLAMA AND ALPACA LEGACY
PERU, ECUADOR, AND BOLIVIA

CHILDREN WITH THEIR ALPACAS IN PERU

Ancient Culture

Quechua (KEH-choo-wah) is one of the most widely spoken native languages in South America. Quechua speakers have lived in South America for thousands of years. Most of today's Quechua speakers live in Peru, Ecuador, and Bolivia. Ancient Quechua speakers, like the Inca, played a key role in domesticating, or taming, the guanaco and the vicuña.

LLAMAS HAVE BEEN USED AS PACK ANIMALS FOR THOUSANDS OF YEARS.

People, Llamas, and Alpacas

Quechua speakers and other people in South America still have a special relationship with llamas and alpacas.

They are used to carry goods and cargo over the mountains (but not too much—an overloaded llama will lie down and not get up until some of its cargo is taken off!).

They are shorn for their wool, which is used to make clothing—both traditional, like the manta (shawl), and modern.

The Inca Empire and the Vicuña

The Inca Empire existed in western South America from the 1300s through the early 1500s. During this time, the vicuña was considered sacred, and people greatly respected this animal. In fact, only royalty were allowed to wear clothing from its wool.

Language

Quechua is still one of the most widely spoken native languages in South America.

You might know these words that come from Quechua:

jerky (dried meat)

puma (another name for a mountain lion or cougar)

condor (a large bird related to vultures, found in parts of South America and parts of the southwestern United States).

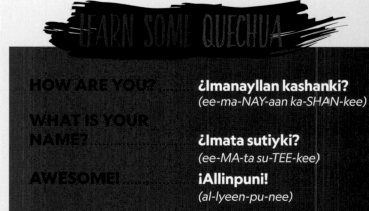

LEARN SOME QUECHUA

HOW ARE YOU?	¿Imanayllan kashanki? *(ee-ma-NAY-aan ka-SHAN-kee)*
WHAT IS YOUR NAME?	¿Imata sutiyki? *(ee-MA-ta su-TEE-kee)*
AWESOME!	¡Allinpuni! *(al-lyeen-pu-nee)*
LLAMA	llama *(That's right, llama is a Quechua word!)*

EUROPE

Europe may be the SECOND SMALLEST CONTINENT, but it has nearly 50 countries! This means that PEOPLE AND ANIMALS OFTEN LIVE SIDE BY SIDE.

I SPENT SOME OF MY CHILDHOOD IN EUROPE—French was actually my first language. The wildlife of Europe played a big part in my decision to be a wildlife vet. The people of Europe work hard—and together—to protect and conserve the environment around them. This care for the outdoors helped INSPIRE MY OWN LOVE OF NATURE and is something I carry with me today.

CLAIMS TO FAME

The oceans north of Europe are home to the **world's LONGEST jellyfish.** The lion's mane jellyfish has **tentacles** that are longer than a **blue whale—** 120 feet (37 m)!

Home to the **LARGEST HERD of reindeer** in the world

Home to one of the **world's RAREST wildcats,** the Scottish wildcat

More than **8,000** species of moths and butterflies

700 species of birds (10 of which are found nowhere else in the world!)

GABBY SAYS!

Doing an exam on an animal that rolls into a ball when it's scared *and* is covered with spines can be a real challenge! When a hedgehog comes in for a checkup, I first put it into a clear glass box, so that I can observe it. Once it starts to relax, it will unroll, and then I can give it a thorough exam—after I put on gloves, of course!

HEDGEHOG

➕ Meet *the Patient*

If you think this little animal looks like it's been stuck through with pins, you're not alone! These spiny mammals aren't related to the prickly porcupine, though. "Hedgies" are most closely related to shrews, a type of small rodent.

♥ Habitat and Family

Hedgehogs live in a remarkable range of habitats: cold, warm, wet, and dry. Some hedgehogs even live in cities! They are solitary animals.

Baby hedgehogs are called hoglets or piglets. Females, or sows, have a litter of four to seven hoglets.

When hedgehogs are born, they are blind; they are also born with a thin sheet of skin called a membrane covering their spines. This membrane dries and shrinks over the next several hours, and then falls away as the babies are groomed. Their soft spines are shed and are replaced by adult spines in a process called quilling.

🍽 Diet

Hedgehogs are omnivores. They eat insects, slugs, snails, frogs, lizards, snakes, vegetables, and fruits.

⚡ Dangers

PREDATORS: raptors, foxes, ferrets, weasels
HUMAN CONFLICT: habitat loss, killing or removal of the animals by people who view them as pests

🔍 Exam Time

SPINES A hedgehog's prickly back is covered with short, spiky spines made of keratin—the same material that makes up your hair and fingernails. When threatened, the hedgehog rolls into a ball, protecting its soft belly.

SPECIAL SHEET OF MUSCLE
A hedgehog has a special muscle on its back. When threatened, this muscle contracts to make its spines stand on end.

KEEN SENSE OF SMELL Hedgehogs have poor eyesight. Instead, they use their strong sense of smell to detect predators. You can see them sniffing the air every few steps when they're on the lookout for danger.

SAVING BABY ANIMALS

Springtime brings babies! And also spring rains. This fox kit had been washed out of its den. Fortunately, someone brought it to the wildlife clinic, where we could give it the care it needed.

THIS LITTLE FOX KIT HAD BEEN WASHED OUT OF HIS DEN DURING THE HEAVY SPRING RAINS. HE WAS DEHYDRATED AND HUNGRY. WE QUICKLY REHYDRATED HIM BY INJECTING SOME FLUIDS BENEATH HIS SKIN AND GAVE HIM SOME SPECIALLY FORMULATED MILK.

One of the best parts for me about being a wildlife vet is saving baby animals. Taking care of babies is much different from caring for adults. We have to take care of any injuries or illness, and also have to provide for their nutritional needs the same way their mother would have.

Mammal babies need milk, while other babies need different forms of food. For example, some species of turtle are exclusively carnivores when babies but will eventually become omnivores, or even herbivores as they grow. Baby frogs (tadpoles) get their nutrients through their water, so I have to make sure their water is clean and has the nourishment they need to grow. Baby birds, depending on their species, might need their food made into mush.

Because every species has different needs, we fine-tune details to make the best breakfast, second breakfast, brunch, lunch, "afternoon tea," supper, dinner, second dinner, midnight snack, and twilight treat for them. It can get complicated. Baby robins, for example, may get more than 100 feedings in a single day!

Finally, we need to make sure that the animal babies "stay wild." It's important that these babies know how to live on their own. First, we make sure that they have as little contact with humans as possible, so that they won't try to approach humans later on.

Second, and as soon as the babies are well enough, we send them to special people called wildlife rehabilitators. (I give them the nickname "rehabbers.") Rehabbers help get the babies ready to return to the wild. They help baby birds gain strength and learn how to fly, and they help them learn how to hunt or find their own food. Working with trained rehabbers is a very important partnership for wildlife veterinarians.

SOMETIMES NEWLY HATCHED SEA TURTLES CAN GET HEATSTROKE AS THEY MAKE THEIR WAY FROM THEIR SANDY NESTS TO THE OCEAN. WE PLACE THESE HATCHLINGS IN COOL WATER TO BRING THEIR BODY TEMPERATURE BACK DOWN. THEN WE GIVE THEM A HEALTH CHECK AND RELEASE THEM BACK INTO THE WILD.

THIS LITTLE LAMB WAS BROUGHT TO THE CLINIC FOR CARE WHILE HER MOTHER RESTED AND RECOVERED AFTER GIVING BIRTH.

EURASIAN BROWN BEAR

➕ Meet the Patient

The brown bear is Earth's second largest bear, and one of the largest carnivores. It's also widespread—although most Eurasian bears are in Russia, you can also find them in the mountain woodlands of Spain, France, and Italy.

♥ Habitat and Family

Brown bears are able to live in a remarkable number of habitats, from mountains to plains, from cold climates to warm. The bears are solitary and strongly discourage other bears from entering their territory. Female bears, or sows, have one or two cubs a year. Cubs stay close to their mother for their first few years while she teaches them how to hunt and defend themselves.

🍽️ Diet

Bears are omnivores and eat smaller animals such as foxes, rabbits, fish, and deer, as well as fruits, berries, roots, and even roadkill.

⚡ Dangers

PREDATORS: other big predators, including tigers, wolves, and other bears

HUMAN CONFLICT: hunting, habitat loss

🔍 Exam Time

LARGE CLAWS A brown bear's claws are mostly for protection and hunting. They're not as sharp as other bears', which is one reason why brown bears aren't good climbers.

MUSCULAR HUMP Brown bears have an extra hump of muscle on their shoulders. This muscle makes them very powerful diggers.

LAYER OF FAT Bears can go into a special state called torpor in the winter. During this time, they don't hunt, don't eat or drink much (if at all!), and don't go to the bathroom—in short, they don't do much of anything that takes energy. They're able to live off the layer of fat they made before they settled down for winter.

WILD FACT!

Not all brown bears are brown—their coats can be a range of colors, from light cream to almost black.

GABBY SAYS!

Humans definitely need regular exercise for a healthy body, but bears, when hibernating, don't. Scientists have found that bears can spend almost half the year dozing and still have a strong heart, muscles, and bones. Scientists aren't quite sure yet how this is possible.

TAIGA

RUSSIA, SWEDEN, FINLAND, NORWAY, AND SCOTLAND

The taiga (TIE-gah) is a huge, cool, evergreen forest. In Europe, taiga covers parts of Russia, Sweden, Finland, Norway, and Scotland. Taigas are also found in North America and northern Asia. You might also hear this biome called "boreal forest," which means "northern forest" or "coniferous forest," because the trees are conifers such as pine trees, firs, and cedars.

OWLS AND OTHER RAPTORS PERCH IN TAIGA PINES AND OTHER CONIFERS.

ANIMALS LIKE MOOSE HAVE ADAPTED TO BE ABLE TO DIGEST THE PLANTS THAT GROW IN THE TAIGA'S POOR SOIL.

WOLVES HAVE THICK, WOOLLY COATS TO KEEP THEM WARM AND DRY WHILE THEY HUNT FOR PREY.

🔥 Fast Facts

» The taiga is one of Earth's biomes. A biome is an area that has a specific climate and physical characteristics and certain plants and animals.

» The taiga's climate can be harsh—winters are cold and snowy, while summers are short and not very warm.

» The soil tends to be thin and rocky, so few kinds of plants can grow.

🐿️ Animal Life

Although the climate here is tough to live in, animals have evolved ways to survive. Animals such as bears and lynxes have thick coats of fur or layers of fat to keep them warm. And herbivores such as moose and reindeer are able to eat the tough, chewy plants that grow in the poor soil.

💬 Taiga Terms

» **conifer:** a tree that stays green all year and whose seeds grow in cones

» **muskeg:** a shallow bog found in North American taiga that forms where water can't drain on the frozen soil and hard rock; mossy and spongy, but looks like solid ground

» **permafrost:** ground that is perma-nently frozen, though the surface may thaw in warmer weather

SOME ANIMALS, INCLUDING BROWN BEARS, SLEEP THROUGH MUCH OF THE TAIGA'S FRIGID WINTERS.

IBEX

+ Meet the Patient

Europe has some truly awesome mountains, including the Pyrenees between France and Spain and the Alps in Germany, Switzerland, and Italy. And where you find mountains, you'll often find herds of wild goats called ibex.

♥ Habitat and Family

Ibex live in small herds. Females and young make up some herds, while males live in their own herds, called bachelor herds.

🍽 Diet

Ibex are herbivores and eat mostly shrubs and grasses. The plants in the mountains aren't always nutritious, so ibex generally spend most of their day grazing to get enough nutrition.

⚡ Dangers

PREDATORS: wolves, eagles, bears, foxes, and lynxes
HUMAN CONFLICT: hunting, loss of habitat

🔍 Exam Time

BUMPY HORNS: Both male and female ibex have long, curved horns, which they use to defend their territory. Male ibex horns can grow up to five feet (1.5 m) long.

POWERFUL LEGS: Ibex can jump up to six feet (1.8 m) into the air with no running start, thanks to their muscular legs. Strong legs also are important for helping ibex keep their balance as they make their way along rocky ledges and cliffs, where they can't be reached by predators.

HELPFUL HOOVES: Ibex hooves are "cloven," or split into two parts like cows' hooves. These split toes have sharp edges, which help ibex climb steep, rocky hills. Their hooves are also concave. That means they bend inward. This shape helps each hoof act like a suction cup, allowing the ibex to do some truly remarkable climbing.

WILD FACT!

An ibex's hoof shape allows it to literally climb walls—and this animal has been known to do so! Ibex often climb the walls of a dam in Italy to lick rocks for the salt they need in their diets.

GABBY SAYS!

Treating animals properly means knowing the difference between things that might look the same, like antlers and horns. Antlers are true bone and are usually shed (fall off) and grow back once a year. Horns are never shed, and are made of bone covered with keratin—so they're always growing.

EURASIAN EAGLE OWL

⊕ Meet the Patient

Europe has 13 species of owls. Stealthy night hunters and fierce birds of prey, Eurasian eagle owls get their name from their large size, which is almost the same as some eagles. These birds are among the largest owls in the world.

♥ Habitat and Family

Eurasian eagle owls live in remote pine forests and grasslands throughout eastern Europe. These owls don't build nests. Instead, they take over nests that other birds have built, or they move into tree holes, stumps, or caves. When a female owl lays eggs, she stays in the nest to tend to them, while the male brings her food and defends the nest.

🍽 Diet

Owls are carnivores and eat insects, mice, birds, rabbits, and other small animals. After an owl finishes swallowing its meal, it throws up what we call casts or pellets. These are made of the bones, fur, and other parts of an animal that the owl can't digest.

⚡ Dangers

PREDATORS: no natural predators

HUMAN CONFLICT: killed by cars and pets

🔍 Exam Time

FANCY FEATHERS An owl has special edges on its flight feathers. These help the owl fly through the air almost silently.

EYES FRONT Having both eyes on the front of its head helps an owl see its prey clearly in low light. An owl can't move its eyes, though. It needs to move its head to see side to side.

UNEVEN EARS An owl's ears aren't evenly set on its head—one is higher than the other. This helps the owl pinpoint where exactly its prey is located.

STRONG TALONS AND SHARP BEAK Owls have a tremendous grip. It takes a huge amount of force to open a clenched talon. Owls hunt with their talons, not with their beaks. But they do use their beaks to tear into their prey.

GABBY SAYS!

The best way to hold these owls during an exam is to firmly hold their feet (usually at the "ankle"), tuck the wings gently under my arms, hold the head gently but firmly, and let it rest the back of its body against my chest. Often, I place a towel over the owl's face, as covering their eyes calms them down. Because these birds have such large and sharp talons, I always use very thick leather gloves to protect myself.

RAPTORS

Raptors are the world's birds of prey. Found on every continent except Antarctica, raptors are set apart from other birds by their sharp beaks and talons, hunting skills, and keen eyesight. Here are some of my favorites, and the dangers they face.

CALIFORNIA CONDOR, NORTH AMERICA

The California condor is one of two types of condors in the world. Once almost extinct, the number of these birds is increasing, thanks to efforts by zoos to raise condors and then release them into the wild to breed.

NORTH AMERICA

CINEREOUS VULTURE, IBERIAN PENINSULA, EUROPE, AND ASIA

Because these vultures tend to eat poison set out for mice and rats, their numbers were once very low—about 800 birds. Thanks to conservation efforts, these majestic birds are breeding again in Spain and Greece, and can be spotted over large parts of Europe and Asia.

GALÁPAGOS HAWK, GALÁPAGOS

The number of these hawks dropped quickly after people moved onto the Galápagos Islands, bringing predators like dogs and cats with them.

SOUTH AMERICA

⚡ Dangers

Because of their larger size and hunting methods, raptors tend to face problems different from those of other birds. For example, raptors often perch in high places to look for prey. If that high place is a utility pole, a raptor risks running into powerlines, which can hurt the bird. While swooping down to grab prey, raptors often collide with trucks, cars, airplanes, and even windmills. Also, like other animals, and particularly because they're on top of the food chain, raptors run a high risk of accidentally eating food that is poisoned or poisonous.

MARTIAL EAGLE, SUB-SAHARAN AFRICA

Known for its massive size and feathered feet, the martial eagle eats a wide variety of small animals. This eagle is often a target for farmers, who hunt the birds to protect their livestock.

⚕ Health

Most of the raptors I see come into the clinic because of run-ins with human-made objects such as cars, fences, and windows. In addition to treating the injured birds, I also do my best to teach others how to solve problems in ways that will keep people happy and raptors safe!

Raptors tend to be at the top of the food chain, meaning that few, if any, animals eat them as prey. But being at the top can create some different problems for these birds.

Because raptors are predators, whatever their prey eats can end up in a raptor's body. For example, if a fish swallows a piece of metal or has absorbed pollution from the water, the raptor that eats that fish might be affected, too. So when we think about helping nature, it's important to think about the whole food chain—not just one part!

WHERE THESE RAPTORS LIVE

- California Condor
- Cinereous Vulture
- Galápagos Hawk
- Martial Eagle
- Seychelles Scops Owl
- Wedge-Tailed Eagle

EUROPE

ASIA

AFRICA

WEDGE-TAILED EAGLE, AUSTRALIA

The wedge-tailed eagle is the largest bird of prey in Australia and a symbol of its Northern Territory. Because they often eat roadkill, they have an increased chance of being hit by cars.

SEYCHELLES SCOPS OWL, SEYCHELLES

The Seychelles scops owl lives mostly on a small island in the Indian Ocean. At one time, the owl was fighting a losing battle with the pets people had brought onto the island, but today its numbers have started to increase.

AUSTRALIA & OCEANIA

WILD FACT! Bats are not blind—they have better eyesight than people do.

GABBY SAYS! Bats are really important to many kinds of flowers. When they travel from flower to flower, they carry pollen, just as bees do. Without bats to carry the pollen, the amount of fruit made by plants can drop—and that can leave other animals hungry.

BATS

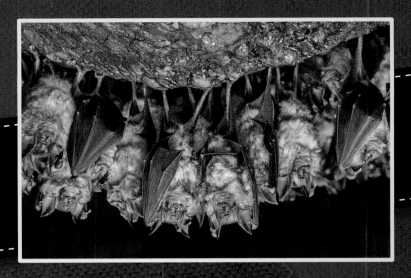

✚ Meet *the Patient*

After years of decreasing, the number of bats in Europe is finally on the rise. This is especially good news because bats have so many important jobs in the environment. For example, they keep insect populations—including pests like mosquitoes—from getting too large.

♥ Habitat and Family

Bats live in large groups called colonies. A colony may live in a cave, a hollow tree, or even the attic of a building. Female bats have one or two babies, called pups, a year. Mother bats are pretty amazing creatures—they give birth upside down! In some species, the babies can fly and hunt on their own at one month old.

🍽 Diet

Different kinds of bats have different diets. Some eat insects, while others feed on nectar from flowers or eat fruit.

⚡ Dangers

PREDATORS: birds of prey such as hawks and owls; snakes; raccoons

HUMAN CONFLICT: fear of bats, diseases such as rabies, pollution, loss of habitat

🔍 Exam Time

FLEXIBLE FINGERTIPS The bones in a bat's wing are similar to our fingers. These bones—which include four fingers and a "thumb"—are super flexible. If you watch a bat in flight, you can see that it doesn't flap its wings like a bird. Instead it pulls itself through the air in a motion that kind of looks like a person swimming.

ECHOLOCATING EARS Some bats find their way around by using echolocation. They send out high-pitched squeaks with their nose or mouth. Then they listen carefully to the sound that comes back.

WING BUMPS Bats have tiny bumps on their wings. Hair in each of these bumps senses the air around a bat and helps it change its wing shape so that it can fly faster.

LEARNING
TO SPEAK BIRD

If you've ever spent time with a human baby, you know that they do and learn different things at different ages. Baby animals are the same way. So an animal's age can have a pretty big effect on how I help it get well. Babies usually get some pretty special treatment.

Once, I found myself having to decide how to take care of a baby crow, or nestling. I was very worried that the nestling would "imprint" on me—that it would learn its behavior from a human (me) instead of learning bird behavior, as it would have from its parents. Imprinting on humans isn't a good thing. Acting like a human wouldn't help the crow very much when it was time for it to go back into the wild. So I needed to keep the crow from imprinting on me.

I thought of a plan: I decided to act as much like a mother crow as I could.

I tried to make my fingers look like a little beak, just like a mother bird would look when she was giving food to her baby. Then, to make the baby think I was a parent bird coming to bring it food,

I would "squawk" at it to try to sound like a crow. To my excitement, the baby immediately stretched its neck up. It had realized that this "squawk" meant "breakfast!"

This little nestling did just great. After a few days of rest, feeding, and care, I tested its blood to make sure it wasn't sick. Once its bloodwork came back normal, we were able to successfully send it to a loving wildlife rehabilitator, who returned it to the wild. It might even have babies of its own someday!

A BABY CROW'S OPEN MOUTH IS A MESSAGE TO ITS PARENTS: "FEED ME!"

CROWS ARE EXTREMELY INTELLIGENT. THEY CAN EVEN TEACH THINGS TO ONE ANOTHER—LIKE HOW TO RECOGNIZE A SPECIFIC PERSON!

LARGE GROUPS OF CROWS SOMETIMES ROOST TOGETHER, ESPECIALLY IN THE FALL AND WINTER.

CAMARGUE HORSE

➕ Meet the Patient

Camargue (CAM-are-GU) horses are small and tough. They're also considered by most people to be the oldest breed of horses in the world, having lived in the marshes of southern France since prehistoric times.

❤ Habitat and Family

Camargue horses live in small herds. A few babies, or foals, are born to each herd each year. The foals are usually dark in color; it takes a few years for their coats to become grayish white.

🍽 Diet

Like all horses, Camargue horses are herbivores. They're not especially picky eaters and can eat the tough, salty, and sometimes smelly plants that grow in salty marshes and swamps.

⚡ Dangers

PREDATORS: wolves, coyotes, and other larger carnivores
HUMAN CONFLICT: none

🔍 Exam Time

NO COLLARBONE: Unlike many other animals, a horse does not have a collarbone, allowing it to make longer strides when it steps. This is one of the reasons that horses are such amazing runners.

EXCEPTIONAL EYES: Horses' eyes are really big—of all of the land animals, only ostriches have bigger eyes. Horses can also move their eyes independently of one another, and they can see almost the whole way around, in all directions.

ONE-WAY STOMACH: Most bigger animals, including humans, can vomit. Horses can't. A piece of muscle called a sphincter controls what goes in and out of an animal's stomach. Once something is in a horse's stomach, their sphincter doesn't let it back out. Scientists aren't sure why, but they think it's to keep horses from throwing up when they're galloping.

WILD FACT!

Adult Camargue horses are always grayish white, but not because they have gray hair! Their color is caused by black skin beneath white hair.

GABBY SAYS!

I get a lot of help when I'm tending to animals in the wild. These particular horses have been domesticated and used for cattle ranching by a group of people called *gardians*. These Camargue horse professionals help round up the herd for yearly health checks.

HORSE HISTORY AND CARE

I could write an entire book on horses—I love them so! And I know I'm not alone. Horses were domesticated thousands of years ago. Since then, they've pulled our carts, helped in our fields, and carried us to faraway places.

Basic Horse Exam

Horses, like all animals, get a thorough exam when I'm around. But there are a few special clues that tell me a lot about how a horse is feeling when I first look at it. Here are three questions I ask myself:

1. How does it look? A horse's coat should be shiny, its head up, and its eyes and nose clear, not runny.

2. What's its attitude? Horses, even the ones that aren't happy to see me, should be alert, and paying attention to people, other horses, and their environment.

3. How is it standing? A horse should be putting weight on all four of its feet. If it's lifting one foot, or shifting back and forth, it might be experiencing a leg or hoof problem.

FROG

HORSESHOE ON HOOF WALL

Hooves

There's a saying among veterinarians: "No hoof, no horse!" A healthy horse starts from the ground up—and that means I take special care to check out a horse's hooves during an exam.

The hoof wall is sort of like your finger- and toe-nails, and it grows throughout a horse's life. It doesn't have any nerves in it, so it doesn't hurt if it gets a trim. It's also the part of the hoof that sometimes has a horseshoe on it. It shouldn't be cracked or split.

The first horses were small—only the size of a dog! Over millions of years, though, horses changed—they got bigger, their legs and muzzles got longer, and their teeth became better at grazing grass. People changed domesticated horses, too, by breeding them for size, color, and strength. Today, there are more than 300 breeds of horses.

EAR

MUZZLE

MANE

KNEE

FETLOCK

BACK

HOOF

FLANK

THIGH

DOCK

WHAT IS A MULE?

A mule has a donkey for a father and a horse for a mother. Mules tend to be stronger and more patient than horses, so people have often used them to carry cargo or pull wagons.

AFRICA

Africa is Earth's

and it is home to some of the

most amazing animals you'll

ever see. The grasslands of

Africa provide food and habitat

to support this animal life. This

and is home to its most famous animals, including

giraffes, zebras, and lions.

Africa is one of the places I visit most frequently,

and it was the site of some of

I was stepping

off the plane on my first trip to Kenya

when I found out I was

About
2,500
kinds of
birds

The
**SMALLEST
butterfly**
in the world—the dwarf
blue butterfly—which
can be less than half an
inch (1 cm) wide

About
1,100
kinds of
mammals

The
**LARGEST
insect** in the world,
the goliath beetle,
which can be over four
inches (10 cm)
long

**Four
of the five
FASTEST**
land animals
on Earth

GABBY SAYS!

At one point there were fewer than 2,500 black rhinos left in the wild. But with people all over the world working together, this number has increased to more than 5,000. Although they are still under threat, it's wonderful to see that conservation efforts have made a difference.

BLACK & WHITE RHINOCEROSES

➕ Meet

There are five species of rhinoceros, and Africa is home to two of them: the black rhinoceros and the white rhinoceros. These two animals have a lot in common, including their *gray* color.

♥ Habitat and Family

Male rhinos are called bulls, females are called cows, and babies are calves. White rhinos live in groups called crashes on the savanna grasslands of southern Africa. Most crashes are small, with only about a dozen animals in them. Typically, black rhinos don't form groups; the only strong relationship formed by black rhinos is between a mother rhino and her calf, which stay together for two to three years.

🍽 Diet

Both black and white rhinos are herbivores, or plant-eaters, but they eat different kinds of plants. Black rhinos hold their heads upright to eat and use their hook-shaped top lip to grab on to leaves and twigs. White rhinos, on the other hand, lower their heads to the ground to chew on grasses and other low-growing plants.

⚡ Dangers

PREDATORS: none

HUMAN CONFLICT: habitat loss, hunting (mostly for horns)

🔍 Exam Time

HARD HORN: The name rhinoceros means "nose" (rhino) "horn" (ceros). The outside of a rhino's horn is covered in something called keratin. You have keratin, too—in your hair and fingernails! Rhinos use their horns to defend themselves, as well as to dig for water.

RADAR EARS: Rhinos have a keen sense of hearing. They can rotate their tube-shaped ears in all directions, like a radar dish, catching even the slightest sound.

SENSITIVE SKIN: A rhino's skin is thick, which protects the rhino from sharp thorns and cutting grasses. But the skin is also sensitive enough that rubbing against each other is a greeting between friendly rhinos. Rhinos wallow in mud to stay cool and to keep biting bugs away. Mud baths also keep rhinos from getting sunburned.

TOUGH TOES: White rhinos can weigh more than 8,000 pounds (3,600 kg), which is quite a lot to carry around all day! Their feet are flat and end in three wide toes. This foot shape helps spread out a rhino's weight and keeps its feet from getting sore and tired.

BLACK RHINO

WHITE RHINO

SAVANNA & FOREST
ELEPHANTS

Meet the Patient

Elephants are some of my favorite animals, and there are a couple types of them in Africa. Savanna, or bush, elephants are the world's largest type of elephant and the world's largest land animal. Forest elephants are smaller than savanna elephants and live in the dense rainforests of west and central Africa.

♥ Habitat and Family

Savanna elephants live mostly on the grasslands found in mid-African countries like Zimbabwe and Namibia. Forest elephants live in warm, wet rainforests around the Congo River in west and central Africa.

Elephants live in herds. Each herd is mostly made up of females (called cows) and their babies (called calves). Each also has a few male (bull) elephants but is led by an older female called the matriarch.

Diet

Elephants are plant-eaters and depend on grass for about 60 percent of their diet. They also are browsers, eating twigs and leaves. And they eat a *lot!* Studies show that elephants eat more than 200 pounds (91 kg) of food every day.

✎ Dangers

PREDATORS: Adult elephants don't have predators, but calves may be prey for lions, crocodiles, or hyenas.

HUMAN CONFLICT: habitat loss and hunting (for their tusks and to keep them off farms)

⚲ Exam Time

MULTI-USE EARS: An elephant's large ears magnify sound, giving the animal excellent hearing, and they also help it stay cool. The large ears give off heat, and as you might have seen, an elephant will flap them gently back and forth, creating a breeze!

FOREST ELEPHANT

FLEXIBLE TRUNK: Both savanna and forest elephants have a long trunk. An elephant's trunk is pretty handy—an African elephant's trunk has two flexible tips that help it pick up objects, squirt water or move dust, dig, or pick up food. Elephants can suck up close to four gallons (14 L) in their trunk in one gulp!

TEETH CALLED TUSKS: Tusks are really just large, long incisors (in-SIGH-zorz), like the pointy teeth in the front of your mouth. Except for their shape and size, they're no different than the rest of an elephant's teeth. Both male and female savanna and forest elephants have tusks. Forest elephant tusks tend to be straighter and point downward, while savanna elephant tusks are curved upward.

SAVANNA ELEPHANT

PADDED FEET: For such a large animal, elephants can move very quietly, thanks to their thick, padded feet. The pads help cushion the bones inside the elephants' legs.

GABBY SAYS!

I love all wildlife, but elephants really are the animal that got me into veterinary medicine. I'm continually fascinated by how they communicate—just by watching an elephant's ears and trunk, I can tell things about its mood and how it's feeling.

THE LUPANI
COMMUNITY SCHOOL
ZAMBIA

ACHIEVING ACADEMIC EXCELLENCE AND PROMOTING SUSTAINABLE CONSERVATION IS OUR FOCUS

LET'S CONSERVE NATURE

IN ADDITION TO LEARNING COMMON SUBJECTS SUCH AS READING AND WRITING, STUDENTS AT THIS SCHOOL LEARN ABOUT CONSERVATION.

A Big Challenge

If there's something I've learned in my travels, it's that living in a big world means living with big problems. When I was in Zambia, I met some kids who are working to solve the big challenges their community faces with wildlife. They're learning about how elephants and other African wildlife use the land around their school—and finding out why it's important to allow some of that land to stay natural, without humans building on or using it.

Elephants face a number of challenges to survival, but one of the biggest is loss of habitat. When their natural habitat is destroyed, elephants are unable to find enough food, water, and safe places to live. By learning how to share the land with their wildlife neighbors, these kids are giving African elephants a real chance to thrive.

Conservation Inspiration

The Sekute community set aside about 50,000 acres (20,000 ha) of land for the conservation of land and animals. Some of this land is essential to the survival of elephants.

Students not only learn about the land and wildlife, they also take care of it by planting and maintaining native vegetation on the school grounds. They learn how to use resources, such as water, sustainably. The school itself runs on solar power!

This school is such an inspiration—it's my hope that other schools and communities can learn from its example and join me and others in helping wildlife.

It is so important to work with animals and equally important to work with the people (especially the young people) who live beside them. The students at Lupani love learning about wildlife conservation. It's such a good, hopeful feeling to know that young people are ready and willing to take on some of the problems we're facing right now!

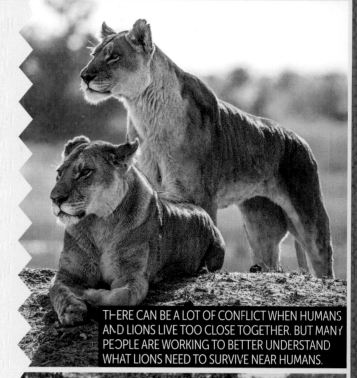

THERE CAN BE A LOT OF CONFLICT WHEN HUMANS AND LIONS LIVE TOO CLOSE TOGETHER. BUT MANY PEOPLE ARE WORKING TO BETTER UNDERSTAND WHAT LIONS NEED TO SURVIVE NEAR HUMANS.

THE SCHOOL GROUNDS WERE DESIGNED TO HAVE THE SMALLEST POSSIBLE IMPACT ON THE WILDLIFE THAT LIVE IN THE AREA.

IMPALAS, LIKE THESE, LIVE ON THE AFRICAN SAVANNA.

Language

Although English is the official language of Zambia, the students who go the Lupani school speak one or more of eight local languages! One of the most common is called Bemba.

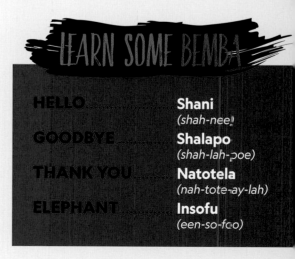

LEARN SOME BEMBA

HELLO	**Shani** (shah-nee)
GOODBYE	**Shalapo** (shah-lah-poe)
THANK YOU	**Natotela** (nah-tote-ay-lah)
ELEPHANT	**Insofu** (een-so-foo)

SHOEBILL STORK

✚ Meet the Patient

Silent, rarely seen, and patient enough to wait for a meal for hours on end, the shoebill stork is a giant, unique-looking bird that lives in the swamps of central Africa.

WILD FACT!

Shoebill storks can (and do) go days at a time without making a sound. But when they do make noise, they make it count! With a din of loud popping and rattling, they warn other animals to stay away from their territory.

♥ Habitat and Family

Shoebills are just one of many animals that live in wetlands like swamps and marshes. These birds almost always live alone, and only come together to mate. The female shoebill will lay one to three eggs at a time. Once the eggs hatch, the female shoebill will raise the chicks until about three months of age, when they are ready to fly.

🍽 Diet

A shoebill's diet consists of mostly fish and small snakes, but it will also eat rodents and even small crocodiles—anything that will fit into its large shoe-shaped beak!

⚡ Dangers

PREDATORS: Adult shoebills have few predators, though their nests may be raided by reptiles and small mammals for their eggs.

HUMAN CONFLICT: habitat loss, hunting

🔍 Exam Time

BARBED BEAK It's easy to spot these curious birds with their large, hooked beaks. The end of the beak is barbed (curves down and forms a hook) and can be used to snag prey from the water.

HUGE FEET Shoebills have really big feet. Their middle toes can be more than seven inches (17 cm) long! The stork's big feet help it stay steady in the mud and water while it hunts.

WIDE WINGSPAN A stork's wings from tip to tip (called its wingspan) can be twice the size of its height—stretching to almost eight feet (2.4m)! Despite their impressive wingspan, shoebill storks aren't powerful fliers. In fact, they don't fly very far or very high off the ground.

GABBY SAYS!

Just because I've gone through veterinary school doesn't mean I've stopped learning. I just recently learned that shoebills are more closely related to pelicans than they are to storks. Knowing how animals are related helps me care for them—especially if I'm treating an animal I've never encountered in person before.

SUSHI
TAKES A BOW

Shoebill storks make their homes in the warm swamps of eastern Africa. People sometimes think they look like a dinosaur, and I can't say they're entirely wrong! They look quite fierce, and Sushi the shoebill stork certainly had a reputation.

I met Sushi the shoebill stork at the Uganda Wildlife Education Center. Sushi is about 30 years old. Shoebill storks can live to be about twice that age, so she's still pretty young—but she's too old to ever go back into the wild.

When birds are very young, they go through something called imprinting. That's when birds learn who to trust and who they should learn from. Usually that's the bird's parents. Because Sushi was taken from the swamp when she was just a baby fledgling, she imprinted on people instead. She trusts people to take care of her. But that could be dangerous to her if she approached the wrong human. She also doesn't get along with other storks, which means she'd have a lot of trouble finding a mate!

Sushi is special—and she knows it! She's not good at sharing, and so has to have a separate enclosure that includes her own pond and pond netting. She's so high-maintenance that she even has her own keeper—taking care of this bird is pretty much a full-time job!

In the wild, if one stork enters another stork's territory, the stork that lives in that part of swamp will defend it, especially if it happens to be a mother shoebill with her chicks. When I work with an animal, I'm always on the lookout for not only the animal's safety but also my own, so I approach every animal I meet very carefully. Knowing that Sushi had a reputation for being a bit difficult, I decided to take some special care introducing myself before getting on with her exam.

THE UGANDA WILDLIFE EDUCATION CENTER IS A REFUGE FOR ALL KINDS OF AFRICAN ANIMALS.

started with my best shoebill stork act! I stood up tall, put out my arms, and tried to make myself look as much like a big bird as possible. My thinking was that if she decided I was bigger than her, she might not go on the attack.

After watching me silently for a few minutes, I was surprised to see that Sushi made a graceful bow! So, I bowed back! And she shook her head as if to say, "You're not doing it correctly," and bowed again. We went back and forth, bowing—until we were "introduced" properly. After this, she allowed me to take a bit of her blood, so I could check and make sure that my new shoebill buddy was healthy.

BEFORE DOING A FULL MEDICAL EXAM, I WALKED ALONG NEXT TO SUSHI, SO I COULD OBSERVE HER BEHAVIOR AND GET A VISUAL CHECK OF HER EXTERNAL BODY PARTS.

HAVING JUST CAUGHT A MEAL, THIS SHOEBILL TAKES OFF FLYING.

GORILLA

✚ Meet the Patient

Gorillas are Earth's largest apes. Although they can seem quite ferocious because of their sharp teeth and powerful build, gorillas are quite shy and gentle. The eastern mountain gorilla is the most endangered of all gorillas.

♥ Habitat and Family

Groups of gorillas, called bands or troops, are often led by a large adult male, the silverback. There may be a few younger males as well, but most of the troop consists of females and their infants. There are about 10 to 20 gorillas in a troop. The world's last remaining troops of mountain gorillas are found in Africa's Virunga mountain range.

🍽 Diet

Gorillas are omnivores, which means they eat both plants and animals. But gorillas eat mostly plants—specifically roots, leaves, tree bark, and fruit. They will occasionally eat a bug or a worm that crosses their path, though. They don't drink much water because they get most of the water they need from the plants they eat.

⚡ Dangers

PREDATORS: none

HUMAN CONFLICT: habitat loss, poaching, and disease (Note: Because gorillas are primates like humans, they can catch diseases from people, but they can't fight them off the way that humans can.)

WILD FACT!

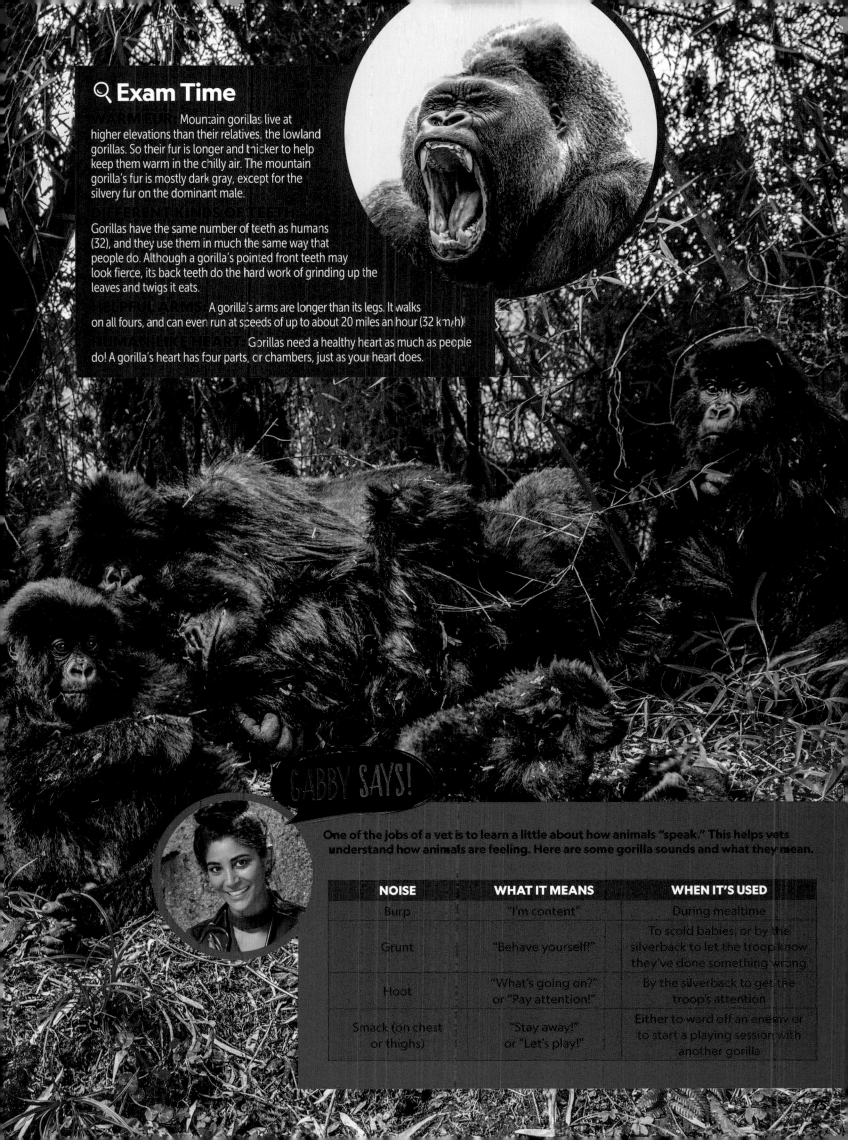

🔍 Exam Time

WARM FUR Mountain gorillas live at higher elevations than their relatives, the lowland gorillas. So their fur is longer and thicker to help keep them warm in the chilly air. The mountain gorilla's fur is mostly dark gray, except for the silvery fur on the dominant male.

DIFFERENT KINDS OF TEETH Gorillas have the same number of teeth as humans (32), and they use them in much the same way that people do. Although a gorilla's pointed front teeth may look fierce, its back teeth do the hard work of grinding up the leaves and twigs it eats.

HELPFUL ARMS A gorilla's arms are longer than its legs. It walks on all fours, and can even run at speeds of up to about 20 miles an hour (32 km/h)!

HUMAN-LIKE HEART Gorillas need a healthy heart as much as people do! A gorilla's heart has four parts, or chambers, just as your heart does.

GABBY SAYS!

One of the jobs of a vet is to learn a little about how animals "speak." This helps vets understand how animals are feeling. Here are some gorilla sounds and what they mean.

NOISE	WHAT IT MEANS	WHEN IT'S USED
Burp	"I'm content"	During mealtime
Grunt	"Behave yourself!"	To scold babies, or by the silverback to let the troop know they've done something wrong
Hoot	"What's going on?" or "Pay attention!"	By the silverback to get the troop's attention
Smack (on chest or thighs)	"Stay away!" or "Let's play!"	Either to ward off an enemy or to start a playing session with another gorilla

VOLCANOES NATIONAL PARK
RWANDA

Located in the northern part of Rwanda, this national park borders national parks in two other countries—Mgahinga (gah-HING-ah) Gorilla National Park in Uganda and Virunga National Park in the Democratic Republic of the Congo. The area containing the three parks is the last remaining habitat for wild mountain gorillas.

FARMING COMMUNITIES CAN BE FOUND BOTH IN AND AROUND THE PARK.

BAMBOO, AN IMPORTANT PART OF A GORILLA'S DIET, COVERS ABOUT 30 PERCENT OF THE PARK'S AREA.

Fast Facts

» Volcanoes National Park was established in 1925.

» It takes up about 60 square miles (160 sq km) of land.

» Part of the park includes five extinct volcanoes.

Plant Life

Bamboo forests cover many of the slopes of the volcanoes. Bamboo is an extremely important resource. It provides food and shelter for many kinds of animals, and it grows very quickly.

Good News

Thanks to the hard work of conservationists and protection by park wardens, the number of mountain gorillas of Volcanoes National Park is increasing every year! We think there are about 1,000 of these beautiful animals now living in the wild.

VISITORS TO VOLCANOES NATIONAL PARK CAN HIKE SOME OF THE SLOPES OF ITS EXTINCT VOLCANOES.

SCIENCE SPOTLIGHT

DIAN FOSSEY was a primatologist who did much of her work in Rwanda's Volcanoes National Park. Primatologists study primates, a group of animals that includes lemurs, monkeys, and apes such as orangutans and gorillas. Fossey founded the Karisoke Research Center to study gorillas and contributed much of what we know about how gorillas interact, what they eat, and where they live. Many people credit the continued existence of mountain gorillas to her dedication to their preservation.

SOME PEOPLE CREDIT DIAN FOSSEY WITH SAVING MOUNTAIN GORILLAS FROM EXTINCTION.

GABBY SAYS!

Because wild dogs are an endangered species, it's important to watch the members to see if they get larger or smaller. To do that, we place a radio collar on the dogs because it can be hard to find them. As a veterinarian, I am able to tranquilize them, check them over, do health checks, and then let them go back into the wild. We hope that by understanding their movements, we can protect their wild habitat.

AFRICAN WILD DOG

✚ Meet

These large dogs with a patchy coat have many names, including painted dogs, hunting dogs, and painted wolves. Once found all over the African continent, their range is now limited mostly to southern Africa.

♥ Habitat and Family

Most wild dogs live on the savanna of Africa, though a few packs have been spotted in African forests. Sometimes these dogs will bed down in dens made and then abandoned by other animals. Like many types of dogs, painted dogs roam in packs with an alpha (head) male dog and an alpha female. Living in packs of about 30 animals, these dogs are highly social, and they will help other animals in the pack. For example, older dogs will let younger dogs eat first.

🍽 Diet

Like all dogs, African wild dogs are carnivores, existing almost entirely on meat. Prey include gazelle, antelope, and wildebeests. They will also eat birds and rodents if bigger game is scarce.

⚡ Dangers

PREDATORS: lions, hyenas

HUMAN CONFLICT: habitat loss, hunting, diseases (including rabies and distemper, often caught from domestic dogs)

🔍 Exam Time

A wild dog's legs are longer and more muscular than many pet dogs'. This helps make them champion runners. They tend to "run down" their prey, chasing it until it gets tired, before going on the attack and dragging it down.

Wild dogs have the teeth of a hunter. They have a long lower tooth on each side of their mouths that is especially good at slicing through meat. The teeth even sharpen themselves as they rub up against the upper teeth.

It's not a stretch to say that most animals don't choose to vomit (throw up). But wild dogs do. Adult dogs will throw up what they've eaten and feed that to their puppies. It sounds gross, but it's how the adults help puppies learn to eat solid food.

LION

⊕ Meet the Patient

The majestic lion has long been nicknamed the "king of the jungle." A better name would be "king of the savanna," since that's where most lions are found.

WILD FACT! They may be bigger, but lions have a lot in common with house cats! They rest for about 20 hours a day.

♥ Habitat and Family

Lions generally make their homes in the same place they find their prey, the African savanna. However, people have also spotted lions in the scrub and woodlands of central and northern Africa.

Lions are the only big cats that hang out in groups. Called prides, these groups can be just a few lions, or up to about 40 cats. Prides generally have only one or two adult males. They guard the territory. The rest of the pride is made up of lionesses and their cubs. The lionesses work together to hunt and raise the cubs.

🍽️ Diet

Lions are carnivores, and prey on almost anything they can find, especially antelope, zebras, wildebeests, and giraffes.

⚡ Dangers

PREDATORS: Adult lions have no natural predators, although they often get into fights with other lions.

HUMAN CONFLICT: loss of habitat, poaching, danger resulting from humans' fear of losing livestock to lions

🔍 Exam Time

FLOWING MANE: Only males have this ruff of flowing hair around their necks. Lions are the only cats whose appearance differs significantly between males and females. The color makes a difference, too. A darker, fuller mane means a strong and healthy animal.

REALLY ROUGH TONGUE: A lion's tongue is covered by small hooked spines called papillae. Lions use these to scrape every bit of meat from bone, as well as to groom themselves. Pet cats have these, too—but a lion could rub your skin raw with just a few licks!

TUFTED TAIL: The tuft of fur at the tip of a lion's tail is unique among the big cats. It's used to communicate with other lions. A lioness may use this tuft as a flag, waving it for her cubs to follow. Beware, though ... a twitching tail often means a lion is in a bad mood!

EYE PATCHES: Lions hunt after sunset, so they need strong night vision. Their eyes have light-colored patches beneath them to help direct any light that's available into their eyes.

GABBY SAYS!

Like many animals, cats have a special surface on the back of their eye, called the tapetum, that reflects light. This is what makes the eyes look like they're shining or glowing. The color in an animal's eyeshine can help you determine what kind of an animal it is. For example, an alligator's eyes reflect a reddish color, while a cat's eyes reflect green.

WILD CATS

Wild cats come in all sizes and colors. They are native to every continent except Australia and Antarctica, and can be found in many different habitats. Despite being able to adapt to many environments, wild cats all over the world face many of the same problems.

NORTH AMERICA

SCOTTISH WILD CAT, SCOTLAND

No one is entirely sure how many of these cats remain in the Scottish Highlands, but most people think there are probably fewer than 100—maybe as few as 35. Because so many people live in Europe, the cat's biggest threat continues to be disease from pet cats.

MOUNTAIN LION, THE AMERICAS

Whether you call it a puma, mountain lion, panther, or cougar, this cat is found throughout most of North and South America. Because it occasionally preys on livestock, it is in almost constant conflict with people.

SOUTH AMERICA

IBERIAN LYNX, SPAIN

Rabbits are the favorite prey of the Iberian lynx. So when the number of rabbits in central Europe dropped because of a disease, the number of lynxes dropped, too. Although the number of Iberian lynx is increasing, the animals are still endangered.

JAGUARUNDI, CENTRAL AND SOUTH AMERICA

These small wildcats are found mostly in South America, but some live as far north as the United States. As with many cats, the jaguarundi faces problems because of habitat loss.

♥ Health

There are hundreds of millions of pet cats in the world. And because they are related to wild cats, they can share their diseases with them. One of the things I always do when I have the chance to treat a wild cat is to make sure that it gets vaccinations for diseases such as rabies and distemper.

Lynxes, bobcats, and other cats that live in the wild are (usually!) bigger than the cats that live in our homes. Sometimes people call any cat that doesn't live with people a "big cat." But scientists use that nickname a little differently. Only tigers, lions, jaguars, leopards, and snow leopards are officially called big cats. Other cats—even ones that look big, like cheetahs—are not included in this group of animals.

WHERE THESE WILD CATS LIVE

- ■ Bengal Tiger
- ■ Iberian Lynx
- □ Jaguarundi
- ■ Leopard Cat
- ■ Mountain Lion
- ■ Scottish Wild Cat

EUROPE

ASIA

AFRICA

LEOPARD CAT, ASIA

Despite their name, leopard cats are not closely related to the much bigger leopard. Their coat shares a similar pattern, though—and they are often hunted for their fur.

BENGAL TIGER, INDIA

The Bengal tiger is one of the biggest living cats, and is the national symbol of India. Like many large wild cats, tigers are sometimes feared by people, and are often hunted as a result.

AUSTRALIA & OCEANIA

⚡ Dangers

Almost all wild cats are protected by law. Unfortunately, people still hunt them for different reasons: for their fur and their use in traditional medicine, and to protect their livestock from the cats.

CHEETAH

✚ Meet the Patient

Cheetahs are the world's land-speed champion, able to go from a stop to 60 miles an hour (96.5 km/h) in about three seconds. Cheetahs have even been clocked running at 70 miles an hour (112.7 km/h) during a hunt. They're considered nearly endangered due to their shrinking numbers.

A YOUNG CHEETAH HAS A FUZZY-LOOKING RUFF ON THE BACK OF ITS NECK THAT GOES AWAY AS IT GROWS UP.

♥ Habitat and Family

Cheetahs can be found in grasslands, deserts, and dry forests. Once found almost everywhere on the African continent, most cheetahs now live in small areas of southern Africa. Mothers and cubs stay together until the cubs are old enough to strike out on their own. Females have three to five cubs per litter, and are very protective of them. Mother cheetahs make chirping sounds to locate their babies that they have hidden in thick grass. Males hang out in groups called coalitions. Often, coalition members are brothers from the same litter.

🍽 Diet

Cheetahs are carnivores, feeding on prey they catch on the savanna. Despite all their running, cheetahs need to drink only every three to four days; they get the water they need from their prey.

⚡ Dangers

PREDATORS: lions, leopards
HUMAN CONFLICT: habitat loss, hunting, poaching for fur and as (often illegal) pets

🔍 Exam Time

BALANCING TAIL: The long tail of a cheetah has an important purpose—it helps it balance while taking turns at high speed. A cheetah can even turn in midair!

CLEAT-LIKE CLAWS: Unlike most cats' claws, a cheetah's claws are always sticking out just a little bit. This helps it to dig into the ground and take off very quickly, and to grip the ground while it's running, the way football and golf shoe cleats work.

STREAMLINED HEAD: The cheetah is built for speed from the head down. The top of its skull is lower than most other cats', making the cat more streamlined, just as race cars are more streamlined than other cars.

FANTASTIC EYESIGHT: Cheetahs have some of the keenest vision of all cats. They have a special part in the back of their eyes that helps them sense even the slightest bit of movement. Cheetahs have black markings beneath their eyes, nicknamed "tear marks," that help reflect the sun, similar to the "eye black" that some sports players put beneath their eyes to reduce glare.

WILD FACT!

Cheetahs are some of the only large cats that don't roar. But they do purr.

GABBY SAYS!

You might have heard that cheetahs run so fast that they sometimes overheat and have to stop. But that's not true. A cheetah's normal body temperature is about 102°F (38.8°C) and rises to about 103°F (39.4°C) after they've been on the run. Your normal body temperature is lower—about 98.6°F (37°C). So a temperature that would be a fever for people is completely normal for a cheetah.

WILD FACT!

These tiny beetles have been observed pushing dung balls more than 50 times their own body weight uphill!

GABBY SAYS!

Dung beetles are one of my favorite examples of how every living thing has an important role to play in keeping the environment healthy. Breaking up dung keeps fly populations from getting too big, and it also helps seeds in the dung make their way into the soil, where they can grow. If it weren't for animals like the dung beetle, everything would get off-balance very quickly.

DUNG BEETLE

➕ Meet

Africa is home to a lot of big animals that leave behind a lot of mess! That dung, or poop, is a home and food source to some kinds of beetles. It may sound gross, but these insects have an important job—cleaning up the environment by breaking down waste.

🔍 Exam Time

Like all insects, dung beetles have six legs. The front legs of male dung beetles have special hooks that help them to grip the ground; the back legs are thin and long enough to roll the ball of dung forward as the beetle walks, its head facing downward.

The head of the dung beetle is wide and flat, like the blade of a shovel. The beetle uses its head to dig a place in the ground for the female to lay her eggs.

Most beetles, including dung beetles, have two pairs of wings. One pair of wings is used to help the beetles fly. A second pair of wings forms a protective shield over the first pair.

💜 Habitat and Family

Dung beetles are active in the summers on African savanna and plains. Like most insects, dung beetles don't spend a lot of time together. However, creating a perfect ball of dung does require the effort of both a male and a female. The male dung beetles gather dung and form it into a ball. When the ball is ready, the male releases a chemical that attracts a female. The female clings to the ball as the male rolls it until they find a soft spot on the ground. They bury the ball together. The female makes a few more balls, laying one egg in each ball. Then she buries the balls beneath the ground to hatch.

🍴 Diet

These insects eat and scatter a lot of dung! Larvae, or baby beetles, eat the solid part of the dung and adults drink the more "liquid-y" part.

⚡ Dangers

PREDATORS: birds, reptiles, amphibians, some mammals

HUMAN CONFLICT: some of the same threats as larger animals (If a bigger animal loses its home to habitat loss, it can't leave any dung behind for the beetles to scavenge!)

CHIMPANZEE

Meet the Patient

Scientifically speaking, chimpanzees are one of humans' closest living relatives. And having spent quite a bit of time with them, believe me—they're pretty similar in how they act, too. Chimpanzees are not monkeys; like gorillas, they are great apes.

Habitat and Family

Chimpanzees live in the warm tropical forests of western and central Africa in groups of males, females, and babies called communities. A community may have more than 100 chimps at a time, though groups tend to join and leave communities. Female chimpanzees usually have one baby at a time, and raise it with a lot of care for up to five years. Sometimes the baby's relatives will even help out when necessary.

Diet

Chimps are omnivores, which means that they eat both plants and animals. Although chimpanzees eat mostly plants, they will also eat eggs and meat ... including meat that's rotting!

Dangers

PREDATORS: young: leopards, other large predators

HUMAN CONFLICT: habitat loss, poaching, disease

Exam Time

OPPOSABLE BIG TOES: All primates (including humans) have opposable thumbs—thumbs that can move across the palm of their hands. Chimps have opposable big toes, too! This allows them to hold, grasp, and open things with both their hands and their feet. A better grasp also means that chimps can use tools to help them to gather food or complete a task.

BIG BRAIN: Chimps have a brain that's big for their body size. They have the brainpower to make decisions and to follow instructions.

WRISTS AND KNUCKLES FOR WALKING: Although they can walk on two legs for a short while, chimpanzees mostly move on all fours. This means walking on the knuckles. A chimp's wrist bones aren't as flexible as a human's, but they are sturdier and better suited for walking than ours are.

GABBY SAYS!

Social bonds are as important to chimpanzees as they are to people—and they make them in a lot of the same ways. You might form strong friendships by hanging out and watching a movie with a group of other people. Well, chimps form bonds by hanging out with other chimps, too. But instead of watching TV, they bond by grooming each other.

WORKING WITH
CHIMPANZEES

One of the ways that chimps are like humans is how they sometimes get into arguments! Well, Rambo got into a little tussle with another chimp and ended up with a cut on his face that got infected. I had to give him some anesthesia to make him sleepy. Then I cleaned up the infection.

We gave him some medicine for the pain. While he was sleeping, I also checked his blood samples for his yearly checkup, and then I did a thorough physical examination.

You can see in the photo that I had a mask on. That was as much for Rambo's protection as mine! Chimps can get sick with a lot of the same illnesses as humans. Illnesses that can be passed back and forth between animals and people are called zoonotic (zoh-uh-NOT-tick) illnesses. The mask was to make sure that poor Rambo didn't catch anything from me!

Fortunately, everything turned out fine for Rambo. His face healed just beautifully. He was one lucky chimp! I was so glad to have met and worked with him.

AFTER WE CLEANED UP THE INFECTION THAT HAD FORMED ON RAMBO'S FACE, WE STITCHED IT CAREFULLY AND GAVE HIM A DOSE OF MEDICINE TO HELP KEEP THE INFECTION FROM COMING BACK. IN THIS PICTURE, WE WERE JUST FINISHING UP THE PROCEDURE.

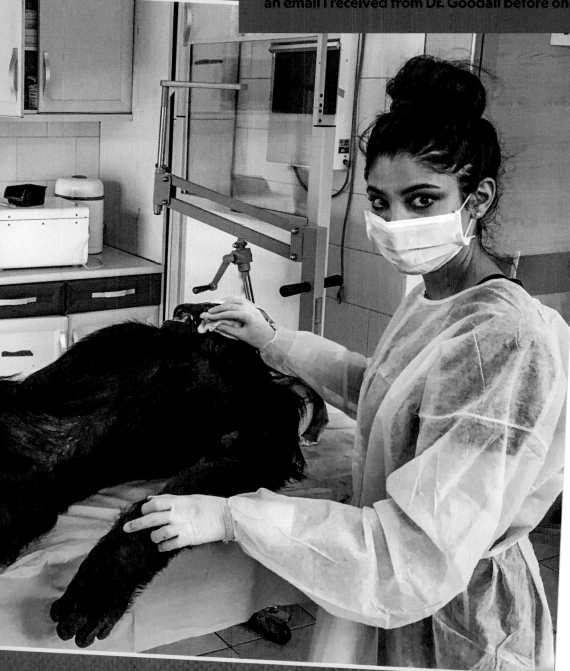

has spent more than 55 years of her life studying and working with chimpanzees in the wild. Much of her work was done in Gombe Stream National Park in the country of Tanzania. By living and working with the chimpanzees that lived there, she was able to discover that they use tools. She found that they act a lot more like humans than people had ever thought. Her work absolutely changed the way that people thought about not only chimpanzees, but also nature and wildlife in general. Her Jane Goodall Institute researches the ways that people can change the environment, and she herself remains active in teaching and inspiring people about nature. Here is an email I received from Dr. Goodall before one of my trips to Uganda.

From: **Jane Goodall**
To: **Gabby Wild**

Dear Gabby,

I was just at Ngamba. You will love it.

I so well remember seeing orphan chimps in what was then Entebbe zoo—now the Entebbe Wildlife Education Centre which I hope you will visit.

Back then, in about 1987 or so, the chimps were in chicken wire cages, terrible conditions, no enrichment, no one who understood them.

And a few adults in strong cages but terrible conditions.

Jane Goodall Institute worked really hard to change all this.

Found a keeper from London zoo who volunteered to help. Her parents paid her fare and got her a secondhand car. Linda Rothen, who became executive director of JGI-Uganda, eventually found Ngamba, and we got the chimps into it when funds had been found.

Luckily for us the government took over the sanctuary (as we already had Tchimpounga and Chimp Eden, and back then, Sweetwaters as well but that also got taken over).

You will love Lilly, the director of Ngamba, and we work closely together.

Good luck!

Warmly,
Jane

WILD FACT! Pangolins seal their nose and ears shut while eating squirmy insects, to make sure none go where they aren't supposed to go.

GABBY SAYS!

Pangolins are one of the most trafficked animals in the world. People poach and hunt them for their unique scales, which some people think can be used as medicine. Fortunately, people in many countries across the globe are banding together to help stop this poaching and to increase the number of pangolins living in the wild.

PANGOLIN

✚ Meet the Patient

When you hear the word "scale," you might picture a fish or a reptile. Pangolins are special in that they are the only mammal that has scales. Four species of ant-eating pangolins live in Africa, all of which have a vulnerable, or nearly extinct, status.

♥ Habitat and Family

Different species of pangolins live in different places. Some live in hollow trees; others dig tunnels and live below the ground. Pangolins like to go solo, coming together only to mate. When baby pangolins are born, their scales are very soft, but they harden over the next couple of years as the animals grow. Babies ride on their mothers' backs for about a month and leave the burrow at about three months.

🍽 Diet

Pangolins don't have teeth, so they are limited to eating only insects. They're especially good at catching ants and termites. Their saliva (spit) is sticky, and the insects stick to their long tongue.

⚡ Dangers

PREDATORS: leopards, hyenas, and large snakes

HUMAN CONFLICT: poaching, habitat loss

🔍 Exam Time

ARMOR OF SCALES A pangolin's scales are made of keratin, the same material as your fingernails and hair. When a pangolin is threatened, it curls up into a ball, using its scales as armor to protect its soft belly. Some people think it looks like a pine cone!

LENGTHY TONGUE A pangolin's tongue is extremely long and thin—that's handy when it's trying to scoop ants and termites out of their holes and hills. Some pangolins are able to stick out their tongues as far as 16 inches (40 cm)! That's in part because a pangolin's tongue isn't attached to the back of its mouth as it is in most animals. It's attached at the bottom of its chest instead.

GRIPPING TAIL Pangolins that live in trees have prehensile tails, like monkeys. They use their tails in the same way, too: to hang upside down. Pangolins can also use their tails to knock away bark from trees, exposing the tasty insects inside.

CLAWS Pangolins have long claws, which they use to dig into soil and bark to find insects.

AMAZING CANINE
SLEUTHS

In addition to working with wildlife in Africa, I work with an organization whose mission is to save wildlife from poaching and illegal trade.

Canines for Conservation is a dog unit in Entebbe, Uganda (with other locations, including Tanzania, in Africa). This unit works with the Uganda Wildlife Authority (UWA) to protect wildlife and monitor illegal trade. Canines for Conservation searches for any potentially illegal animal products, including rhino horns, elephant tusks, pangolin scales, antelope horns, snakeskins, crocodile skin, and hippo teeth.

The dogs are our super sleuths. They use their amazing sense of smell to follow the trail of poachers or of the wildlife they might be poaching. The dogs sniff all products being imported (brought into) and exported (sent away from) the country, as well as all travelers' suitcases. I help this organization by taking care of the dogs as their veterinarian and training the dogs' handlers on basic medical procedures in case of an emergency. The handlers sometimes even video chat with me from thousands of miles away when they have a question about their dogs' health. I'm happy to do what I can to make sure these dogs can keep doing their important work.

CANINES FOR CONSERVATION SENDS DOGS TO AIRPORTS AND SEAPORTS ALL OVER AFRICA.

NOBODY CAN INTERPRET WHAT A DOG IS TRYING TO "SAY" BETTER THAN ITS HANDLER—THEY TRULY HAVE A SPECIAL RELATIONSHIP.

SOME BREEDS OF DOGS CAN SNIFF SCENTS THAT ARE SEVERAL WEEKS OLD!

WHY USE SNIFFER DOGS?

A dog's nose is much more sensitive than a human's. Dogs have over 300 million receptors in their nose, while we have only about six million. A bigger portion of a dog's brain (compared to a human's) is dedicated to figuring out what a smell is, too.

ASIA

Asia is home to a huge variety of habitats, from the MOUNTAINS OF NEPAL to the DESERTS OF CHINA and MONGOLIA. Thousands of interesting animals live here, including the RED PANDA, JERBOA, and PIT VIPER.

I've loved elephants since I was a child, and I got to meet them in their natural habitat when I was 16 years old! I FIRST WENT TO THAILAND to learn as much as I could about elephants and their behavior. I also began learning how to work with elephants and even about elephant medicine.

CLAIMS TO FAME

Earth's LARGEST amphibian, the Chinese giant salamander

Earth's SMALLEST bat, the bumblebee bat, which grows to be about two inches (5 cm) wide.

Home to what many consider the only **true WILD horse:** Przewalski's horse

Earth's SMALLEST bear, the sun bear, many of which are only about the size of a large dog!

Earth's LONGEST snake, the reticulated python

GABBY SAYS!

Red pandas have a sweet tooth. The red panda's tongue, like the human tongue, has different types of taste buds. Scientists discovered that red pandas have taste buds that help the animals taste aspartame (an artificial sugar). That was a surprise! Scientists had thought that only primates (like monkeys and people) could taste artificial sugars.

RED PANDA

+ Meet the Patient

Red pandas may share part of a name with the well-known giant panda, but they're not related to them at all. These colorful animals of central China share a family with weasels, raccoons, and skunks.

♥ Habitat and Family

Red pandas live most of their life in thick forests, sleeping in the branches, and only coming down when necessary. They spend most of their time alone, meeting only to mate. Mother red pandas have a litter of two to four cubs, which go off on their own once they are a year old.

🍽 Diet

Like the giant panda, red pandas eat a diet of bamboo shoots and leaves. However, they've also been known to eat fruit, flowers, eggs, and even small birds.

⚡ Dangers

PREDATORS: snow leopards

HUMAN CONFLICT: habitat loss, hunting, poaching for fur

🔍 Exam Time

FIERY FUR: Red pandas live in areas that have plenty of red mosses and white or gray lichens. The reddish and white coat of a red panda helps it blend in with its surroundings.

SPECIAL PAW PARTS: Part of the red panda's front paw forms something like a thumb. Although it's not exactly the same as your thumb, it has the same function and helps the panda grip tightly on to trees as it climbs.

FLUFFY TAIL: No blanket, no problem! The red panda's thick fur helps keep it warm and dry in the snow. And if it does get cold, it simply wraps up in its large tail to keep warm.

WILD FACT! Captive red pandas are well-known escape artists—they have managed to escape zoos in Washington, D.C., England, and the Netherlands.

AMUR LEOPARD

✚ Meet the Patient

Leopards are found in more countries around the world than any other big cat. Amur leopards, though, are the rarest of all leopards. We think there are fewer than 60 Amur leopards left in the wild.

♥ Habitat and Family

Amur leopards live in the temperate rain- forests of the Russian Far East and China. These shy creatures spend most of their time alone, making it hard to learn much about them. We think that male leopards may help raise their cubs, which is a bit unusual among the big cats.

🍽 Diet

Amur leopards eat mostly deer, hares, badgers, and wild pigs. They are patient hunters and will stalk their prey, following and watching it closely before attacking.

⚡ Dangers

PREDATORS: Wolves and tigers may prey on younger leopards.

HUMAN CONFLICT: habitat loss (80 percent of their habitat is gone), poaching for fur, hunting

🔍 Exam Time

STRONG SHOULDERS: The neck and shoulder muscles of leopards are especially strong. This makes leopards some of the strongest and best climbers of all the big cats. They'll even drag their prey up into a tree!

CREAMY, SPOTTED COAT: A leopard's distinctive pattern of spots is called rosettes because the spots are arranged in a way that looks a little bit like a flower. The Amur leopard has wider-spaced rosettes and a paler shade of fur than other leopards. This coat color helps it blend into the back- ground, especially in areas of spotty shade.

MUSCULAR LEGS: Leopards are great leapers, and can leap to a spot more than 20 feet (6 m) away and 10 feet (3 m) straight up!

WILD FACT!

These leopards like their leftovers—Amur leopards will hide anything they don't eat so that other predators don't take it.

GABBY SAYS!

When the numbers of an animal living in the wild get as low as the Amur leopard's, we have to be extra careful to watch them for illnesses. For example, a thorough exam helped us find the form of distemper normally found in dogs, even though leopards are cats.

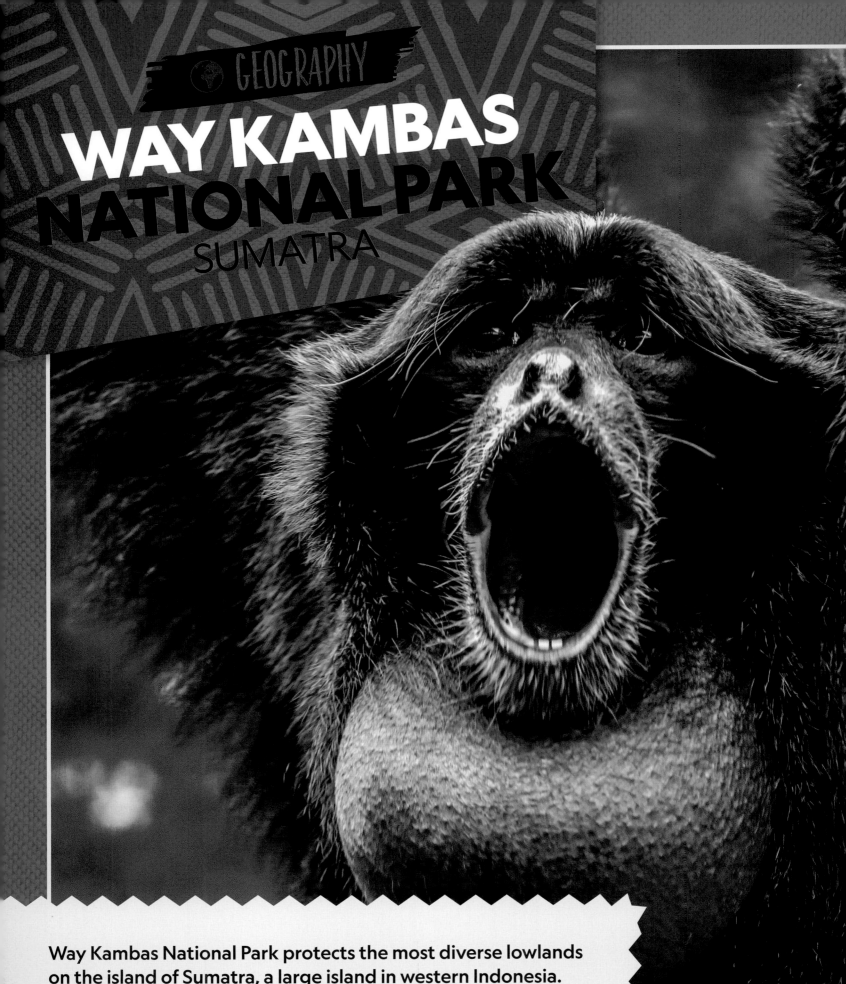

WAY KAMBAS
NATIONAL PARK
SUMATRA

Way Kambas National Park protects the most diverse lowlands on the island of Sumatra, a large island in western Indonesia. Mostly rainforest, the park is home to elephant and rhino sanctuaries. Dholes, a type of wild dog, scout for prey on the forest floor, and gibbons called siamangs swing above. Many of the species here are found almost nowhere else on the planet.

A SIAMANG'S LARGE THROAT SAC HELPS ITS CALL BE HEARD UP TO TWO MILES (3.2 KM) AWAY.

THE MIDDLE PART OF A CORPSE FLOWER CAN GROW TO BE 10 FEET (3 M) TALL!

THIS KINGFISHER IS JUST ONE OF OVER 400 SPECIES OF BIRDS THAT LIVE IN THE PARK.

THE PARK SERVES AS A SANCTUARY FOR ANIMALS LIKE THE SUMATRAN RHINO.

🍃 Fast Facts

» Sumatra is the sixth largest island in the world.

» The high amount of rainfall and tropical temperatures on the island create an environment filled with lots of different wildlife, including elephants, rhinoceroses, and tigers.

🌿 Plant Life

Sumatra is home to some incredible plants, including the gigantic titan arum. This plant, also known as the corpse flower, is known for its putrid smell when it blooms. Luckily, that only happens every two to 10 years. While the odor can be sickening to humans, it smells like dinner to flesh flies and carrion beetles.

⭐ Good News

Resources on an island are limited. If a disease destroys an island plant species that an animal needs for food, the animal can't just move to another place. So it's important to take special care of all the life on the island.

SUMATRAN RHINOCEROS

✚ Meet the Patient

Sumatran rhinos are the smallest kind of rhino, the most vocal, and the hairiest! But like the rest of the world's rhinos, they are endangered. There are only about 100 of them left in the wild.

♥ Habitat and Family

Sumatran rhinos live in Sumatra's dense rainforests, as well as those in Borneo and Malaysia. These animals live alone—if you see two together they are likely a mother and her calf. They're also especially good at marking their territory and will even break apart and twist the branches and trunks of young trees to let other rhinos know to keep out.

🍽 Diet

Sumatran rhinos are herbivores. Like black rhinos, they are browsers, munching on leaves, twigs, and young trees. They love fruit when they can get it, and they eat about 10 percent of their body weight every day.

⚡ Dangers

PREDATORS: none

HUMAN CONFLICT: poaching for horns, habitat loss

WILD FACT!

The Sumatran rhino is the closest living relative to the extinct woolly mammoth.

🔍 Exam Time

FAST FEET: Sumatran rhinos are especially fast on their feet (at least compared to other rhinos). Their feet are also well adapted to climbing steep hills and mountainsides.

HARD HEAD: Breaking through rainforest branches isn't a big challenge for this rhino. In addition to its horns, it has a hard ridge of skin around its head to help it make its way through the brush.

HELPFUL HAIR: This coat does the opposite of keeping the rhino warm! Mud and dirt stick to the hair, keeping the rhino cool and bug-bite free.

GABBY SAYS!

Munching on tough tree branches can be hard on teeth. Older rhinos can have an especially hard time chewing their food. So when I work with rhinos in zoos and conservation centers, I make sure to check out each rhino's bite to see how worn its teeth are. If they're too worn down, we can change the animal's diet to make sure it doesn't go hungry.

SPYING ON WILDLIFE

Sumatra is a hot spot of biodiversity. It is teeming with many different kinds of plant and animal life, and in some cases, life that is found in no other place in the world. It has more animals than any other island in Indonesia.

Later, we watch the video clips. We identify any animals we see, and we count them. We try to figure out how many of each species are still in the wild. Then we share what we find, so that other people—including scientists, veterinarians, and conservationists—can keep track of what's going on.

But many of the animals here are endangered. Their numbers have been dropping fast over the past few decades, and keeping count of the remaining populations is key to helping them regrow. So, how can we tell how many animals are left on the island? My amazing friends and I are working hard to protect wildlife there by placing cameras around the rainforest to monitor the area. Sometimes we even catch poachers. The cameras work by taking small clips of video. We put the cameras in places we know wildlife will be—around water, for example.

THE PART OF THE CAMERA TRAP THAT MAKES A COCOON AROUND THE SPOTTER IS MADE OF NATURAL MATERIALS LIKE ROPE. THESE MATERIALS WILL BIODEGRADE, OR BREAK DOWN, AND WE LEAVE NO TRACE ON THE ENVIRONMENT.

IT'S ALWAYS A THRILL FOR ME TO SEE AN ANIMAL CAPTURED BY A CAMERA IN THE WILD!

MANY ANIMALS ARE ON THE MOVE AFTER DARK, SO THE CAMERAS WE USE HAVE NIGHT-VISION TECHNOLOGY.

GABBY SAYS!

When working in zoos, we are often able to train orangs to be still during a checkup. However, if they need, say, their blood pressure taken or their heart checked out more thoroughly, I will make sure that they are given a bit of anesthesia. It's very important that we monitor heart health, as orangutans (and great apes in general) can often get heart disease.

ORANGUTAN

✚ Meet the Patient

Found only in Borneo and Sumatra, critically endangered orangutans spend almost all of their time in the trees. Sometimes called "orangs," these red apes are gentle and intelligent.

♥ Habitat and Family

Orangutans are especially suited for life in the rainforest. They spend much of their time in trees, and make their nests out of leaves. Unlike gorillas and chimps, these apes spend a lot of time alone, although they will occasionally travel in small groups from place to place.

🍽 Diet

Orangutans are omnivores and will eat both plants and other animals. Fruit is a special favorite—an orangutan's diet tends to be mostly sweet fruits, with occasional meals of leaves, insects, or eggs.

⚡ Dangers

PREDATORS: tigers, leopards, and crocodiles
HUMAN CONFLICT: habitat loss

🔍 Exam Time

FATTY FLANGES: Some male orangutans have cheek pads called flanges. These puffy pads, made mostly of fat, help differentiate some adult males from others. Males with these flanges also have a throat sac that makes the animal's call loud enough to be heard across large areas of rainforest.

LONG ARMS: Orangutans can give really big hugs! A male orangutan's average arm span can stretch seven feet (2.1 m) from fingertip to fingertip. This long span is suited to a tree-living lifestyle, allowing the animal to easily swing from branch to branch.

FLEXIBLE HIPS: An orangutan's hips are much more flexible than most other primates'. Because of this, they can use their legs to vault from tree to tree. And as they move, their arms are free for other tasks, like gathering food.

WILD FACT! Orangutans are really good at solving problems. They've been observed building roofs over their nests to stay dry during a rain shower.

PRIMATES

Primates are a group of mammals that includes monkeys, apes, lemurs, humans, and more. Wild, nonhuman primates are found on every continent except Australia and Antarctica. Many primate species need protection to keep their numbers from declining further. Here are some examples of animals in need of help.

NORTH AMERICA

SOUTH AMERICA

BARBARY MACAQUE, GIBRALTAR

Fewer than 250 monkeys live on Gibraltar, a rocky point on Spain's southern coast. They are the only wild monkeys that live in Europe. Most Barbary macaques live close by in northern Africa.

MEXICAN SPIDER MONKEY, YUCATAN

Although much of their original habitat is now farmland, spider monkeys can still be spotted swinging nimbly from tree to tree in southern Mexico.

BLACK-FACED LION TAMARIN, BRAZIL

Tamarins are tiny—many are only about the size of a squirrel! Some species, such as the black-faced lion tamarin, only live in a small area, so they are particularly sensitive to habitat loss.

MANDRILL, CONGO

Mandrills are the world's largest monkey. The male mandrill, with its bright red and blue face, is also the most colorful mammal on the planet.

⚡ Dangers

No matter where they live, many of Earth's primates share the same threat: habitat loss. Logging or burning trees to clear land for farming or development forces animals to move into smaller and smaller areas. The primates also lose their sources of food and other things they need to survive.

Monkeys and apes are often confused with each other, but they're not the same. Apes do not have tails, tend to live on the ground, and exhibit more intelligence than monkeys. We put monkeys into two groups: New World and Old World. New World monkeys live in North and South America; Old World monkeys live mostly in Asia and Africa.

WHERE THESE PRIMATES LIVE

- Barbary Macaque
- Black-Faced Lion Tamarin
- Lemur
- Mandrill
- Mexican Spider Monkey
- Proboscis Monkey

EUROPE

ASIA

AFRICA

PROBOSCIS MONKEYS, BORNEO

The word "proboscis" is often used to refer to a long tube or snout of an animal, such as a butterfly's or elephant's—and that is definitely how this monkey got its name! These Old World monkeys share the rainforests of Borneo with orangutans.

🩺 Health

Because humans, monkeys, and apes are all primates, monkeys and apes can get a lot of the same diseases as humans. When I encounter primates in the wild, I make sure to give them vaccines for diseases like measles and the flu.

AUSTRALIA & OCEANIA

LEMURS, MADAGASCAR

There are 100 different kinds of lemurs—and they are all found in only one place! Lemurs make their homes on the island of Madagascar. These primates have noses that are always moist, much like a dog's nose.

ASIAN
ELEPHANT

✚ Meet the Patient

At first glance, Asian elephants might seem to be almost identical to African elephants, but they're actually quite different. Asian elephants are smaller than their African relatives, and they're different in other ways, too!

WILD FACT! Despite living in a tropical environment, Asian elephants do not have sweat glands—so they often take a dip in mud or water to keep cool.

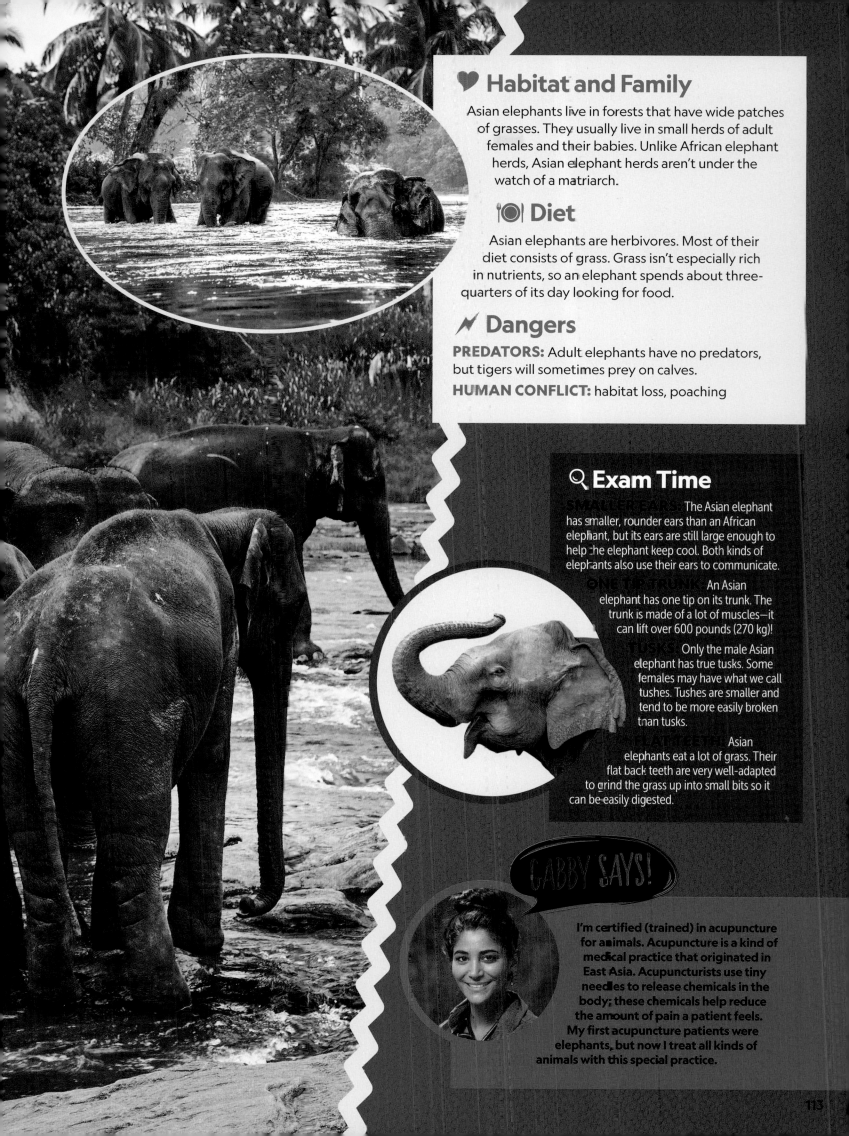

♥ Habitat and Family

Asian elephants live in forests that have wide patches of grasses. They usually live in small herds of adult females and their babies. Unlike African elephant herds, Asian elephant herds aren't under the watch of a matriarch.

🍽 Diet

Asian elephants are herbivores. Most of their diet consists of grass. Grass isn't especially rich in nutrients, so an elephant spends about three-quarters of its day looking for food.

⚡ Dangers

PREDATORS: Adult elephants have no predators, but tigers will sometimes prey on calves.

HUMAN CONFLICT: habitat loss, poaching

🔍 Exam Time

SMALLER EARS: The Asian elephant has smaller, rounder ears than an African elephant, but its ears are still large enough to help the elephant keep cool. Both kinds of elephants also use their ears to communicate.

ONE TIP TRUNK: An Asian elephant has one tip on its trunk. The trunk is made of a lot of muscles—it can lift over 600 pounds (270 kg)!

TUSKS: Only the male Asian elephant has true tusks. Some females may have what we call tushes. Tushes are smaller and tend to be more easily broken than tusks.

FLAT TEETH: Asian elephants eat a lot of grass. Their flat back teeth are very well-adapted to grind the grass up into small bits so it can be easily digested.

GABBY SAYS!

I'm certified (trained) in acupuncture for animals. Acupuncture is a kind of medical practice that originated in East Asia. Acupuncturists use tiny needles to release chemicals in the body; these chemicals help reduce the amount of pain a patient feels. My first acupuncture patients were elephants, but now I treat all kinds of animals with this special practice.

113

KHUN CHAI

Khun Chai was "my" baby elephant, and he is the reason why I do everything I do. I've always loved wildlife, as well as the sciences, nature, the outdoors, and animals. And this was all good, because you have to like the sciences, as well as animals, to be a vet. But Khun Chai was truly the animal that inspired me to be the person I am today.

When I was 16, I was able to spend some time working in Thailand with elephants. I started as a trainer, learning all I could about elephant behavior. Before I was allowed to work in the elephant hospital, I had to be able to understand elephants, their care, and how to work with them. So I went back year after year to work with the elephants. Finally, I was ready to be a hospital assistant.

By this time, I was 21 and finishing college. That's when I met my baby elephant, Khun Chai. He had been stolen from his mother in the rainforest. In Thailand, they often use elephants as farmwork animals. And a farmer thought he could take the baby and train it himself. He thought this would be a lot cheaper than buying a trained elephant. Little did he know, though, that the baby really needed its mother. It wasn't getting enough nutrition and

became so sick, it was close to dying. The farmer realized that the baby needed medical help.

He took it to the hospital where I had been working. There, Khun Chai had a difficult time. He didn't want to play with other elephants. He didn't want to interact with people. He did finally learn to love an older female elephant, and she became kind of a stepmother to him. But sadly, during the rainy season, she slipped and died in a mudslide. Khun Chai was left all alone again, and he was very, very depressed. He was so depressed that he wouldn't eat. He ate enough to just barely survive, but he was sick. He needed calcium. He needed milk.

This was Khun Chai's state when I arrived at the hospital. The staff asked me to go see him, thinking maybe Khun Chai might like me. A lot of tourists would come up to Khun Chai because he was so cute, but he would completely ignore them. I had studied some elephant behavior, so I knew that he just wanted to be left alone. So when I went into his enclosure, I just sat there quietly. And when I looked at him, it was just out of the corner of my eye—I didn't want him to know that I was paying attention to him. About 30 minutes later he came up to me and tapped me with his trunk. He realized that I was the only person who didn't give him too much attention! From that moment on, we were inseparable. Khun Chai became my baby. He would follow me around everywhere. The villagers would call me his "stepmother." In fact, I couldn't get too far ahead of him, or he would be upset!

I would feed him milk five times a day and walk him three times a day. I bathed him every three days. Slowly, he got better. In the meantime, at the hospital, we decided that because he had been around people so much it would be dangerous to release him back into the wild. We decided it would be best for him to stay at the local conservation center instead. There, he would have a protected, "semi-wild" life, and he would be able to occasionally interact with people. His job would be to teach visitors about Asian elephants and why we need to protect them. He certainly taught me plenty.

KHUN CHAI AND I WOULD TAKE WALKS TOGETHER IN THE MORNING AND AFTERNOON.

THAILAND AND ELEPHANTS

A National Symbol

The elephant is the national symbol of Thailand and is deeply woven into the history of the country. White elephants in Thailand were once considered a symbol of royalty and were given as gifts between kings. To some people in Thailand, the elephant is a sacred animal and a symbol of strength and wisdom. The elephant also is featured in many of Thailand's stories and poems.

ELEPHANTS ARE FEATURED IN ARTWORK OF ALL KINDS IN THAILAND.

Elephants Today

For many years, wild elephants were caught and tamed in Thailand for use in logging. Elephants are no longer used for this purpose—commercial logging has been outlawed in Thailand since 1989. Elephants that had lived in captivity relied on people for their care and could not return to the wild. A new tourism industry emerged in response. Today, about 3,800 elephants live in captivity. Many of them live in camps, performing tricks and giving rides to tourists. Some organizations are working to create sanctuaries for captive tourism elephants, where the animals can roam peacefully but still live under human care. However, the tourism industry makes a lot of money, and so many new elephant babies are still trained for this kind of entertainment. Tourists can help change the future for elephants, though, by choosing to pay for more natural, elephant-friendly sanctuary experiences instead.

A Serious Situation

In countries where wildlife is a big draw for tourists, as in Thailand, we often see "wildlife tourism" experiences offered to visitors. These experiences provide tourists opportunities to take photos with—or even ride on—the wild animals, which are held in captivity. While it may seem like a supercool experience for people who love these animals, the animals are often kept in less than ideal conditions and can be mistreated. Luckily, groups are working to ensure ethical treatment of these animals, including improving their living conditions and discouraging tourists from visiting such sites.

ALTHOUGH THE ROLE OF ELEPHANTS IN THAILAND HAS CHANGED, THEY ARE STILL AN IMPORTANT SYMBOL TO THE COUNTRY'S PEOPLE.

ELEPHANTS HAVE A SPIRITUAL SIGNIFICANCE TO MANY PEOPLE IN THAILAND.

Language

Thai is the official language of Thailand. Like some other languages, Thai has words that may look the same in writing but can have different meanings based on how they're pronounced.

LEARN SOME THAI

HELLO AND GOODBYE .... **sawatdi-kha**
(if spoken by a girl;
swa-dee-KAAAH
or sawatdi-khrap
(if spoken by a boy)
swa-dee-KAP
The greeting usually goes along with the wai,
a slight bow with the palms pressed together.
ELEPHANT .... **chang**

117

BACTRIAN CAMEL

✚ Meet the Patient

Larger and hairier than the Arabian camels of Africa, most Bactrian camels live and work with people in a manner very similar to horses in other parts of the world. About 950 wild Bactrian camels, however, live in the deserts of eastern China.

GABBY SAYS!

There's a way to tell if a camel is getting nervous and ready to spit: The corners of its eyes start to wrinkle (we call it the "worry wrinkle"), and the pouches of its mouth begin to bulge a little bit as they fill with spit and stomach juices. If that happens ... it's time to get out of the way!

♥ Habitat and Family

In addition to deserts, camels live in rocky mountains and plains. Wild camels live in herds of about 20 individuals, usually with one male, or bull, camel taking charge. Younger bulls stay near their mothers, and help to raise young calves until they're about five years old. Then they take on their own herd.

🍽 Diet

Camels are herbivores, and mostly eat shrubs and grasses. In a pinch, though, these camels can munch on plants that are thorny, dry, or even salty. They also drink a lot of water, gulping down up to 30 gallons (114 L) of water in only 13 minutes.

⚡ Dangers

PREDATORS: wolves

HUMAN CONFLICT: habitat loss, poaching for meat

WILD FACT!

Wild Bactrian camels can drink water that's somewhat salty—something that's dangerous for many other animals.

🔍 Exam Time

TWO HUMPS Bactrian camels have two humps. These humps don't store water. But they do store fat, which can be used for energy if a camel doesn't get enough to eat.

LOTS OF LONG EYELASHES Sand is very bad for any animal's eyes. So camels have not one but two rows of extremely long eyelashes that help keep out the tiny, irritating grains of sand.

WIDE FEET Camels walk on their toes, which can spread far apart. Having a wide foot helps keep a camel from sinking into the soft soil or sand.

SMELLY SPIT When camels are surprised or irritated, they throw up a little bit. They mix this vomit with the saliva in their mouths ... and spit it at whatever is bothering them.

SHAGGY COAT Winters can be very cold in the desert. So these camels grow a thick, shaggy coat in the winter to keep warm.

SIBERIAN TIGER

➕ Meet the Patient

Siberian tigers are the largest cats on Earth! Unlike the tigers that live in the tropical jungles of southern Asia, these tigers like the cold and snow. Siberian tigers live in small areas of northern China and eastern Russia.

♥ Habitat and Family

Like most cats, Siberian tigers don't care much for company, preferring to live alone. Female tigers have litters of two to six cubs, and tend to them for up to three years. After that, they're on their own.

Diet

These tigers are fierce carnivores and can eat more than 200 pounds (90 kg) of meat per week. Prey usually include elk and other deer, as well as wild pigs, but Siberian tigers have been known to go after bears or wolves. They hunt by sneaking up on their prey almost silently before pouncing.

⚡ Dangers

PREDATORS: none

HUMAN CONFLICT: habitat loss, hunting for pelts or sport

🔍 Exam Time

FUR: A tiger's stripes help it hide in tall grasses and brush. Each tiger has a unique stripe pattern on its face, and only males have the tufts of fur on their cheeks.

FAT LAYER: Although a tiger's fur helps it stay warm, it also has a fairly thick layer of fat under its skin. Siberian tigers' homes can get as cold as minus 45°F (-43°C)!

MASSIVE BODY: Tigers are one of the only cats that are too heavy to climb. However, they are excellent jumpers and can jump more than 15 feet (4.5 m) into the air to grab prey out of a tree.

WILD FACT!

Stripes fade as a tiger gets older—younger tigers have more stripes than older tigers.

GABBY SAYS!

Wildlife vets not only look at animals as individuals but also at how they interact with their ecosystem. Recently, a very deadly disease called canine distemper virus—which is found in a wide range of carnivores (and famously, in dogs)—was discovered in wild Amur leopards. We worried about the leopards becoming sick, and because they share territory with these rare tigers, we now worry that the tigers will come down with the disease, too.

WILD FACT! Qinling pandas are giant pandas, too, but they aren't black and white. Their fur is light and dark brown.

GABBY SAYS!

Most animals that rely heavily on plants in their diet have a complex stomach and large cecum (a pouchlike structure at the beginning of the large intestine). Not giant pandas! They have a digestive tract much like other kinds of bears—one that's adapted to digest meat. So, as much as they love to munch on bamboo, they're not great at digesting it. That's why they spend up to 14 hours a day eating!

GIANT PANDA

✚ Meet the Patient

The giant panda is one of the most easily recognized animals in the world, not only for its black and white coloring, but also because of efforts aimed at its conservation. It's also a widely known symbol of China.

♥ Habitat and Family

Pandas live in the bamboo-forested mountains of China. Adult pandas live alone and defend their territory from intruding pandas. Cubs stay with their mothers until the next cub is born or for about two years.

🍴 Diet

Giant pandas live the life of an omnivore. Although they exist almost entirely on bamboo plants, they occasionally also eat fish, small reptiles, and eggs.

⚡ Dangers

PREDATORS: Like other bears, adult pandas have no natural predators; jackals, leopards, and martens (a type of weasel) may prey on panda cubs.

HUMAN CONFLICT: habitat loss, poaching

🔍 Exam Time

STRONG JAW: The panda's friendly-looking round face is actually the result of extremely powerful jaw muscles. It needs them to tear and grind up the bamboo shoots that make up most of its diet.

UN-BEAR-LIKE TEETH: Like most other bears, which eat mostly meat, pandas have sharp front teeth. But a panda's molars are bigger than most bears', which helps the panda carefully chew the bamboo it eats.

SIXTH TOE: Giant pandas have an extra toe that helps them grip bamboo stems tightly.

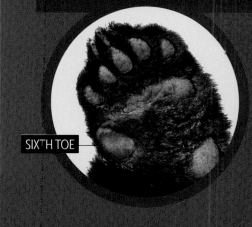

SIXTH TOE

AUSTRALIA & OCEANIA

Oceania is a **WORLD REGION** that includes Australia, New Zealand, part of New Guinea, and hundreds of smaller islands in the **PACIFIC OCEAN.** It is also home to many of the **WORLD'S MOST EXTRAORDINARY ANIMALS.**

New Zealand, made of a collection of islands, has more than **50 VOLCANOES**—and that's just part of what makes this country an amazing place to work.

The **PARROTS, MARSUPIALS,** and **MONOTREMES** (like the platypus) that live here are really **UNIQUE** compared to many of the other animals I work with. Because they're so **DIFFERENT,** they can have health problems that are different from what I usually see, too. But I'm always up to meeting the challenge!

CLAIMS TO FAME

140 species of **land snakes**

About **32** species of **sea snakes**

The **giant weta,** one of the world's **LARGEST INSECTS,** weighing **three times** more than a **mouse**

Animals that **exist** in the **WILD here** and nowhere else

The only **TWO mammals** that lay eggs—the platypus and the echidna

MARVELOUS

MARSUPIALS

KANGAROOS ARE ONE OF THE WORLD'S MOST FAMOUS MARSUPIALS.

Australia is home to most of Earth's marsupials (mar-SOUP-ee-allz). Marsupials are a special group of mammals.

Marsupials can be small, like shrews, or large, like kangaroos. Some—the opossum, for example—can tolerate the chilly winters of North America, while others, like the bilby, are adapted to life in the hot Australian desert. Marsupials can live entirely in trees, on the ground, beneath the ground in burrows, or even partially in water.

So what do all these animals have in common? The answer lies in how marsupials have their babies. Most mammal mothers carry their babies inside their bodies until they're pretty big. Marsupial babies are born when they're very tiny, and before they've finished developing.

The tiny marsupial babies immediately crawl into a special pouch on their mother's belly. There, these "pouch young" drink their mother's milk and grow bigger and bigger. Warm and protected in their mother's pouch, they grow until they're developed enough to leave the pouch and become "joeys." Joeys spend the next few months climbing in and out of their mother's pouch, learning about the outside world. They climb back into their mother's pouch to feed, rest, and warm up. Eventually, the young marsupials have enough fur and are old enough and big enough to live on their own outside the pouch.

BABY KANGAROOS ARE ABOUT THE SIZE OF A JELLY BEAN WHEN THEY'RE BORN.

WOMBATS, LIKE THIS ONE, HAVE A POUCH THAT IS UPSIDE DOWN—IT OPENS TOWARD ITS HIND LEGS INSTEAD OF ITS HEAD.

BY ABOUT SIX MONTHS OF AGE, KOALA JOEYS ARE BIG ENOUGH TO BE ON THEIR OWN

GABBY SAYS!

A mother koala helps her joey eat leaves by digesting them for her baby. Instead of spitting the food back up as some animals do, the mother produces pap, a special kind of poop made just for the little one to eat.

KOALA

⊕ Meet the Patient

These cuddly-looking animals look a lot like bears, but they're not bears at all. Like many Australian animals, they're marsupials. They're not especially cuddly, either—they're actually quite fierce for their size!

♥ Habitat and Family

Koalas live in forests where there are a lot of eucalyptus trees. They're not friendly at all with other koalas and are often quick to fight each other. This is especially true for males, which are called bucks. Female koalas, called does, usually have one joey at a time. Once the joey is big enough to be on its own, its mother will drive it away.

🍽 Diet

Koalas almost exclusively eat the leaves of eucalyptus trees. These leaves don't have a lot of nutrition in them, so koalas eat a lot and digest them slowly. They get almost all the water they need from these leaves, so they don't need to drink very often.

⚡ Dangers

PREDATORS: Dingos and pythons prey on adults. Raptors like hawks, eagles, and owls prey on joeys and small koalas.

HUMAN CONFLICT: climate change, habitat loss, run-ins with pets such as dogs

🔍 Exam Time

TWO-SIDED COAT: A koala's fur is longer and darker on its back and shorter and lighter on its belly. The long, dark fur soaks up the sun's heat and repels rain and wind. The short, light fur reflects sunlight and helps keep the animal cool. So what does a warm koala do? Flop over to expose the short, light fur to cool off, of course.

AMAZING DIGESTIVE SYSTEM: Eucalyptus leaves are toxic (poisonous) to most animals (including people!). Koalas can eat them because one part of their digestive system breaks down the poison. There's also a big pouch in the koala's large intestine that helps it break down the tough, leathery leaves.

BUM PAD: Because koalas spend a lot of time sitting and sleeping in trees, they have a pad of cartilage (like the wiggly tissue in your nose) at the bottom of their backbone that helps keep them comfortable.

SUPERSPECIAL CLAWS: Koalas have different kinds of claws. Some are good for grabbing and gripping branches to nibble or climb. Others are used for grooming themselves.

WILD FACT! Koalas burn energy at a very slow rate. They move very slowly. They're also real pros at napping. They snooze for about 18 hours every day!

KANGAROO

✚ Meet the Patient

The kangaroo is one of Australia's most recognizable symbols—and with good reason! For every human living in Australia, there are two kangaroos. There are four species of kangaroos in Australia, but the biggest are the red and the gray.

♥ Habitat and Family

Kangaroos live wherever grasses and other plants are plentiful, usually in groups of 10 or more called mobs. Male kangaroos are called bucks (though Australians call them boomers or jacks). Females are called does (but are nicknamed flyers or jills).

🍽 Diet

All kangaroos are herbivores, although different species eat different kinds of plants. Grasses, shrubs, and even certain kinds of mushrooms are on the menu, depending on the species.

⚡ Dangers

PREDATORS: Kangaroos have no natural predators.

HUMAN CONFLICT: climate change, habitat loss, danger posed by cars, cats, and dogs

🔍 Exam Time

TOUGH TAILS Kangaroos use their big tails for balance as they leap across the ground. They also use their tails to push off from the ground when they're moving at slower speeds.

SPRINGY STEPS 'Roos have some big leg muscles, but a lot of their hop comes from body parts called tendons, which attach their muscles to their leg bones. These tendons are very stretchy, and they act like a spring, putting even more bounce in a kangaroo jump.

TONS OF TEETH Grass can be tough on an animal's teeth and can wear them out quickly. Kangaroos are one of the few animals that are constantly growing new teeth to replace the old. This is called "molar progression."

ALL-SEEING EYES (ALMOST) Kangaroos can see really well to their left and right. In fact, they can see movement in almost every direction. Their binocular vision also enables them to see things clearly up close (just as we can).

RED KANGAROO

GRAY KANGAROO

WILD FACT!

Many animals will sweat whenever they get hot. Kangaroos sweat only after exercising. If they're hot but not exercising, they will pant or lick their arms to cool down.

"SIR, DID YOU SAY 'KANGAROO'?"

When you're out in the field helping wild animals, you learn to expect almost anything—and you usually get it!

When I first started training as a wildlife vet, I was "on call" for my wildlife clinic. The clinic is located in the state of New York, and our job was to take care of all wild animals that live in the area.

One evening when I was on call, a man called the hospital frantically needing to speak to the wildlife doctor. That was me! So the receptionist transferred his phone call to my mobile phone. The man was very upset. He was talking very quickly and was in tears. I did my best to calm the man down so he could speak clearly.

Finally, he muttered, "Doc, I need help. My kangaroo hit his head." I thought I had heard him incorrectly, so I asked him to repeat what happened. "Doc, it's my kangaroo!" I cleared my throat and politely said, "Sir, did you say 'kangaroo'?" He had, and it was his kangaroo that he was calling about.

The man had permission to keep several kangaroos because he used them for education. This little kangaroo had gotten into a fight with another kangaroo. The other kangaroo had hit him hard enough to knock him over, and he had hit his head.

The man brought his poor little red kangaroo into the clinic. After an examination, I treated the kangaroo for a bump on the head. A day later, he had recovered beautifully.

I never expected to see a kangaroo at a wildlife clinic more than 10,000 miles (16,100 km) from Australia! But you never know when you're going to put your experience to good use.

IT'S NOT UNCOMMON FOR KANGAROOS TO SPAR, OR FIGHT, DURING PLAY.

DON'T BE FOOLED BY THE FUZZ—
EVEN YOUNG KANGAROOS LIKE
THIS ONE LEARN TO FIGHT ...
FIRST WITH THEIR MOTHER, THEN
WITH OTHER YOUNG 'ROOS.

PARROTS

There are almost 400 different kinds of parrots. They range in size from large kakapos and macaws to tiny pygmy parrots. Parrots need warm temperatures to survive and are found on every continent except Antarctica. Here are some of the species that are endangered.

THICK-BILLED PARROT, MEXICO

This parrot, which nests on cliffs in Mexico, is the only surviving parrot native to North America. The other, the Carolina parakeet, has been extinct since 1918. People are working to save these birds by ensuring they have plentiful food and nesting sites.

NORTH AMERICA

AFRICAN GRAY PARROT, CONGO

Most of the African gray parrots kept as pets were not taken from the wild. As a result of poaching and habitat loss, however, the number of African gray parrots in the wild is low enough to keep the species on the list of endangered animals.

LAWS HELP

In 1992, the United States passed a law making it illegal to capture wild parrots to keep them as pets. Since then, the number of birds taken from the wild has dropped!

SOUTH AMERICA

♻ Health

Parrots can be difficult to live with. They are not always friendly and can be quite noisy. Some frustrated pet owners let their parrots go, which is a dangerous practice. If the parrots are able to survive, and have babies, they can become an invasive species in an area. Invasive species cause harm to their new environment by eating food and using resources needed by other kinds of animals.

LEAR'S MACAW, BRAZIL

Lear's macaws are fussy about their habitat. They like to roost in one specific type of palm tree. As people cleared land for farming, many of these macaws lost their homes. At one point, there were only 60 left in the wild, but today, thanks to conservation efforts, we think there are well over 1,000.

⚡ Dangers

Parrots are colorful, intelligent birds. Many are able to imitate sound, including human voices. These qualities make them popular as pets. Unfortunately, taking parrots illegally from their habitats causes harm to their ecosystem, the parrot population across the world, and the parrot itself.

PARROT FARMERS

Parrots have an important role to play in their habitat. This is because they do two things. They eat fruit and seeds and they fly. Because seeds often pass through a parrot's digestive system without being broken down, the seeds eventually come out in the bird's poop. As a result, parrots plant seeds for fruit and flowers every time they poop. By doing so, they're keeping the forests where they live healthy and growing for a long time.

WHERE THESE PARROTS LIVE

- African Gray Parrot
- Blossom-Headed Parakeet
- Lear's Macaw
- Orange-Bellied Parrot
- Thick-Billed Parrot

EUROPE

ASIA

AFRICA

BLOSSOM-HEADED PARAKEET, THAILAND

At one time, the blossom-headed parakeet was one of the most popular pets in Europe. Known for forming large, loud flocks, this endangered species lives in the forests of India and Thailand.

ORANGE-BELLIED PARROT, AUSTRALIA

The orange-bellied parrot is one of the only kinds of parrot that migrates, flying to another area of Australia to breed and raise its young. Zoos in Australia are breeding these parrots and releasing them into the wild in an effort to increase their numbers.

AUSTRALIA & OCEANIA

WILD FACT!

Kakapos may not fly, but they're great climbers! They'll climb to the top of a tree, and leap off, using their small wings like a parachute to help them land safely on the ground.

GABBY SAYS!

Kakapos are one of my favorite birds, but they are not always the easiest parrots to work with. For example, they are very sensitive to being hospitalized and often get stressed. They can become so stressed at the hospital that they won't eat enough. So veterinarians need to feed the birds extra food with a tube to make sure they get enough nutrition. This extra feeding can go on for several weeks.

KAKAPO
PARROT

✚ Meet the Patient

Kakapos are the world's heaviest parrots. These big, round birds live on the oceanic islands that make up the country of New Zealand. Once almost extinct because of habitat loss and new predators—the cats, rats, and other animals that Europeans introduced—today the kakapo population has been increasing, thanks to a lot of hard work and cooperation.

♥ Habitat and Family

Kakapos prefer to live in grasses and scrublands near rocky coasts. Kakapos are fighters and will attack other parrots they encounter. Male kakapos gather in an area and perform for the females in a display called "lek." They each dig a shallow hole in the dirt and make a loud booming call. The female chooses the male she likes best and then lays one or two eggs in the hole. The chicks will stay with their mother until they are about six months, before going off on their own.

🍽 Diet

Kakapos are mostly herbivores, snacking on native plants, seeds, fruits, pollen, and tree sap. Because they don't fly, kakapos don't use as much energy as other birds, so they don't need to eat very much.

⚡ Dangers

PREDATORS: cats, rats, ferrets, weasels

HUMAN CONFLICT: habitat loss, pets that prey on kakapos

🔍 Exam Time

ROUNDED WINGS: Because kakapos don't fly, their wings look different from those of other parrots. They're smaller and rounder in shape.

SMALLER MUSCLE: Most birds have strong chest muscles to help them fly quickly or over long distances. Kakapos have these muscles, too ... but because they spend so much time walking, they're much smaller.

FUNKY FACIAL FEATHERS: Kakapos have special feathers around their beak. They use these feathers the way some other animals use whiskers—to find their way around in the dark.

THE FIRST NEW ZEALANDERS

A FORM OF DANCE CALLED POI INVOLVES SWINGING WEIGHTS THROUGH THE AIR.

Home Sweet New Zealand

The Maori were the first people to live in Aotearoa (the native word for New Zealand). Today, about 17 percent of people living in New Zealand identify with this cultural heritage. Caring for family and community is an important part of Maori culture, and their culture emphasizes a strong connection to both one's ancestors and to the tribal lands that have been held for generations.

Kakapo parrots are special birds to the Maori people of New Zealand. Historically, kakapo feathers were used by or given to only chiefs and other people of high status in the community. Maori also traditionally traded the birds like money and kept the friendly birds as pets.

WOMEN PERFORMING A HAKA

Maori Arts

Carving is a special Maori tradition. Artists pay their respects to the past by creating detailed masks and other works of art. What may look like lines are actually stories meant to be read by others.

Another tradition is the haka, or ceremonial dance. Haka is performed by a group, and uses chant and rhythmic foot stomping to share a particular message. It is traditionally performed to welcome guests or on special occasions.

SPIRALS, CIRCLES, AND TWISTS ARE COMMON SHAPES FOUND IN MAORI CARVING.

WEAVING IS USED TO MAKE ALL SORTS OF OBJECTS, INCLUDING BASKETS AND SOME KINDS OF CLOTHING.

SOME MAORI STILL GET A SPECIAL FORM OF TATTOO CALLED TA MOKO.

Language

The native language of the Maori, Te Reo Maori, was only spoken, not written, for hundreds of years. It probably wasn't until the 19th century that the language was recorded in written form.

The number of people who speak Te Reo Maori is declining. It's estimated that less than 20 percent of the Maori speak this language today.

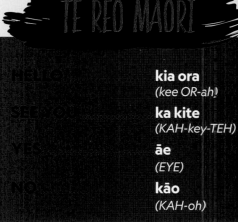

LEARN SOME TE REO MAORI

HELLO	kia ora (kee OR-ah)
SEE YOU	ka kite (KAH-key-TEH)
YES	āe (EYE)
NO	kāo (KAH-oh)

OCTOPUS

➕ Meet the Patient

I'm often asked what is the weirdest animal that I've treated. I guess I'd have to say one of the oddest creatures is the octopus. Octopuses are related to other mollusks like snails and clams—but they have a lot more personality!

♥ Habitat and Family

Most octopuses make their homes by building a rocky den along a reef or on the seafloor. Octopuses aren't like many other sea creatures, which hang out in groups. Instead, octopuses are generally found alone. Females will lay their eggs in a sheltered spot, and then guard them, keeping them clean and safe until they hatch.

🍽️ Diet

Octopuses like to eat shrimp, crabs, lobsters, and clams—but they'll eat fish if they can get them.

⚡ Dangers

PREDATORS: large fish, mammals like seals and whales
HUMAN CONFLICT: habitat loss, overfishing, pollution

🔍 Exam Time

STRONG SUCKERS: Each of an octopus's eight arms is lined with suckers that the octopus uses to grab and hold on to things. In some species, each individual sucker can lift 35 pounds (16 kg)!

SPEED BY SIPHON: Octopuses can jet away from predators by squirting water through a muscular tube called a siphon.

DO-IT-ALL MOUTH: An octopus's mouth has different parts that do different things. It has a hard beak (rather like a parrot's) that breaks shells, a spiky tongue called a radula used to scrape the flesh out of the shell, and a tooth-covered organ that drills into shells if the beak or tongue methods don't work. It also releases a secretion that breaks down the shell of its prey to weaken it so that it can then be eaten.

THREE HEARTS: These animals have not one, not two, but three hearts! Two pump the blood through the gills to help the animals breathe, while the third sends blood throughout the body.

WILD FACT! Octopuses have a special sac in their body that fills with a dark chemical. If an octopus is attacked, it lets this ink out of its body, leaving predators in a dark cloud while the octopus makes its getaway. The ink also gives the octopus extra time to flee: It prevents the predator from smelling or tasting the water, confusing it further.

GABBY SAYS!

How do you tell if an octopus is sick? It doesn't get the sniffles or a fever. Usually, one of the first signs that an animal isn't feeling well is when it stops eating. In the case of one female octopus I treated, I knew she was sick because even though she should have been in her egg-laying stage, she had stopped laying eggs. A vet really needs to be a detective and pay attention to different kinds of clues.

THE GREAT
BARRIER REEF
AUSTRALIA

Although I mostly treat land animals, I do sometimes help out with aquatic ones, including seahorses, fish, octopuses, and other sea-dwelling creatures. Many of these animals live on or near coral reefs.

The Great Barrier Reef is the world's largest coral reef. It's about 1,615 miles (2,600 km) from end to end, and can be seen from outer space! It's also home to a tremendous number of living things.

THE REEF

CORAL REEFS ARE PLACES OF HIGH BIODIVERSITY, MEANING LOTS OF DIFFERENT TYPES OF LIVING THINGS, LIKE THESE CRESCENT-TAIL BIGEYE FISH, LIVE THERE.

CORAL BLEACHING OCCURS WHEN OCEAN WATERS GET TOO WARM—A WELL-KNOWN EFFECT OF CLIMATE CHANGE.

CLOWNFISH AND SEA ANEMONES ARE JUST TWO ANIMALS THAT COUNT ON EACH OTHER TO SURVIVE ON THE BARRIER REEF.

✿ Fast Facts

» Some scientists consider the Great Barrier Reef the largest living thing on the planet.

» Six species of sea turtles come to the reef to breed.

» About 30 kinds of sea mammals, such as whales, dolphins, and dugongs, have been spotted around the reef.

🌿 (Not) Plant Life

Corals may look like plants or flowers, but they're animals. They also have a special relationship with algae, tiny organisms that live inside the corals. The algae use energy from the sun to make food that the corals use. In return, the corals provide some of the nutrients the algae need to stay healthy. But if the water gets too warm, or if it gets polluted, the algae start to make chemicals that are poisonous to the corals. In turn, corals force the algae out. But without these algae, the corals lose their color. Scientists call this coral bleaching. Coral bleaching can lead to corals dying off.

SCIENCE SPOTLIGHT

MANY ZOOS HAVE AQUARIUM EXHIBITS that include a small coral reef for visitors to view. As a wildlife and zoo vet, one of my jobs is to make sure that the animals in these tanks are healthy. One of the first things I'll do is test the water to make sure it's clean and has enough oxygen. Then I check for diseases—they can spread quickly in water. Sometimes just putting medicine right in the water will prevent the spread of illness.

SCRUB PYTHON

✚ Meet the Patient

One of the longest snakes in the world, the scrub python can grow to be more than 24 feet (7 m) long. These reptiles play an important role in their ecosystem by controlling the number of rodents in their area.

GABBY SAYS!

These snakes get into special kinds of veterinary trouble. I've read about a case in which a scrub python swallowed a stuffed toy cow and had to have it removed by surgery!

144

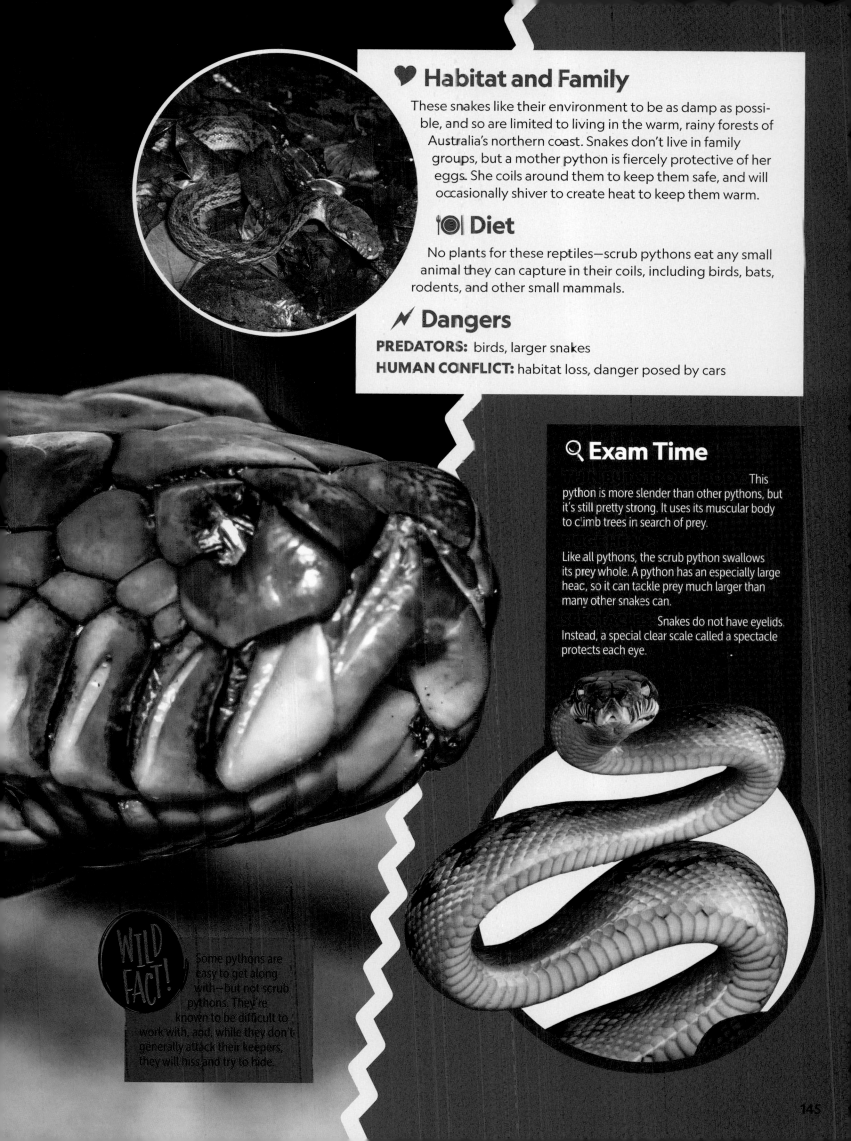

♥ Habitat and Family

These snakes like their environment to be as damp as possible, and so are limited to living in the warm, rainy forests of Australia's northern coast. Snakes don't live in family groups, but a mother python is fiercely protective of her eggs. She coils around them to keep them safe, and will occasionally shiver to create heat to keep them warm.

🍽 Diet

No plants for these reptiles—scrub pythons eat any small animal they can capture in their coils, including birds, bats, rodents, and other small mammals.

⚡ Dangers

PREDATORS: birds, larger snakes
HUMAN CONFLICT: habitat loss, danger posed by cars

🔍 Exam Time

This python is more slender than other pythons, but it's still pretty strong. It uses its muscular body to climb trees in search of prey.

Like all pythons, the scrub python swallows its prey whole. A python has an especially large head, so it can tackle prey much larger than many other snakes can.

Snakes do not have eyelids. Instead, a special clear scale called a spectacle protects each eye.

WILD FACT! Some pythons are easy to get along with—but not scrub pythons. They're known to be difficult to work with, and, while they don't generally attack their keepers, they will hiss and try to hide.

A SCARY (BUT LUCKY) SNAKE SITUATION

I have a little confession: I'm afraid of snakes. But that doesn't mean I don't take care of them and that I don't love them. All animals are beautiful and need our help!

A bunny had been hit by a car and was on its way to the clinic. As soon as it arrived, I knew it had to be taken into the back of the hospital—into our "exotics ward," where animals of all sorts are watched overnight—so I could get to work treating it.

As I was racing to open the cabinets and grab supplies, I looked down to see two beady eyes staring back at me … and I let out a bone-shattering scream! Never did I expect that one of the exotic ward patients was a 20-foot (6-m)-long python!

Luckily, the python, named Betty, was in a special cage designed to give her extra oxygen. But poor Betty and the poor bunny had to deal with my very loud scream. After I calmed down, I was able to take good care of the bunny, which had a broken leg. With lots of attention, it made a full recovery … and was kept in a totally different area of the hospital so as not to be petrified of a snake that normally would consider her a nice little meal!

There's more to the story, though. It was a bit of good luck that I came to the clinic that night,

SNAKES ARE EXTREMELY IMPORTANT PREDATORS IN MANY ECOSYSTEMS.

because Betty was not doing very well. After making sure the bunny was okay, I decided to gather my courage and have a look at Betty.

The big snake's breathing was a little bit off, and she had what appeared to be a very runny nose. I noticed that she seemed to be getting worse. I quickly called the vet who had been taking care of her and told him about the situation. We decided to give her additional medicine, and that helped her get better!

SCIENTISTS THINK THAT A SNAKE'S VERTICAL PUPILS HELP IT TO SEE ITS PREY CLEARLY IN LOW LIGHT.

PART OF THE REASON THAT A SNAKE CAN SWIM IS ITS LONG, THIN BODY, WHICH SPREADS ITS WEIGHT OUT EVENLY IN WATER.

PLATYPUS

✚ Meet

When scientists first saw this animal, they thought someone was trying to trick them. The platypus is an interesting-looking animal, with its duck-like bill and webbed feet—and it lays eggs! But, because it has fur and nurses its young, it's still considered a mammal.

PLATYPUSES DON'T HAVE TEETH, SO THEY HAVE TO SCOOP UP GRAVEL WITH THEIR MEAL, LIKE THIS WORM, TO HELP GRIND UP THEIR FOOD.

♥ Habitat and Family

The platypus lives in Tasmania and along the east coast of Australia, in both cool and warm streams and rivers. Platypuses live alone in burrows, and come together only to mate. The female platypus lays two or three eggs and keeps them warm with her tail. A baby platypus is only about the size of a lima bean, and drinks its mother's milk for three or four months before leaving the burrow.

🍽 Diet

The platypus is a carnivore, feeding on insect larvae, worms, and small shellfish from the bottom of rivers. It stores its food in cheek pouches until it comes back to the surface, where it eats its catch.

⚡ Dangers

PREDATORS: crocodiles, snakes, raptors such as hawks and owls

HUMAN CONFLICT: habitat loss, getting caught in nets and traps meant for other animals

GABBY SAYS!

Vet exams sometimes mean taking some blood from an animal for tests. You may have seen a veterinarian take blood from your own pet's front or back leg. With a platypus, it's easiest to get blood from the front of its bill!

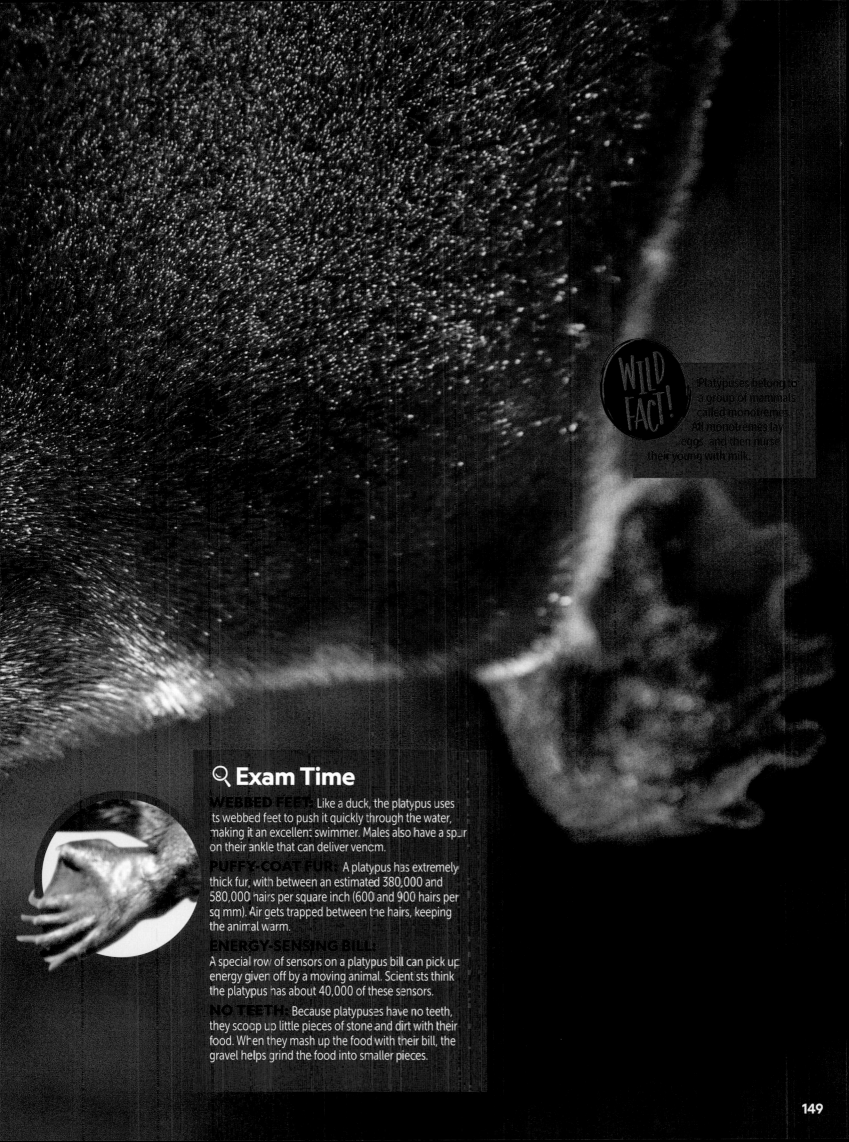

Platypuses belong to a group of mammals called monotremes. All monotremes lay eggs, and then nurse their young with milk.

🔍 Exam Time

WEBBED FEET: Like a duck, the platypus uses its webbed feet to push it quickly through the water, making it an excellent swimmer. Males also have a spur on their ankle that can deliver venom.

PUFFY-COAT FUR: A platypus has extremely thick fur, with between an estimated 380,000 and 580,000 hairs per square inch (600 and 900 hairs per sq mm). Air gets trapped between the hairs, keeping the animal warm.

ENERGY-SENSING BILL: A special row of sensors on a platypus bill can pick up energy given off by a moving animal. Scientists think the platypus has about 40,000 of these sensors.

NO TEETH: Because platypuses have no teeth, they scoop up little pieces of stone and dirt with their food. When they mash up the food with their bill, the gravel helps grind the food into smaller pieces.

NORTH AMERICA

North America is **MY HOME BASE.** When I'm not off working in the field with wild animals, I'm seeing patients in an animal clinic in the United States. North America contains **MANY DIFFERENT ECOSYSTEMS,** from the icy plains of northern Canada to the tropical forests of Mexico and the Caribbean islands.

New York State is where I did most of my studying to become a veterinarian. It's where **I LEARNED SO MUCH ABOUT BEING A WILDLIFE VET.** I spent many years working daily with **NORTH AMERICAN WILDLIFE,** including red-tailed hawks, porcupines, and squirrels!

CLAIMS TO FAME

Close to **1,000** species of birds

Everglades National Park, home to **two BIG reptiles:** crocodiles and alligators

20 species of venomous snakes

Hawaii, where most of its animals **(9 of every 10)** are found nowhere else on Earth

The HEAVIEST members of the deer family— moose!

BALD EAGLE

➕ Meet the Patient

Bald eagles can be spotted soaring in the skies above most of North America. Once almost extinct in the United States, the numbers of bald eagles have been on the rise, thanks to people working together to protect these beautiful and majestic birds.

♥ Habitat and Family

Bald eagles tend to spend most of their time alone but will sometimes roost and build nests in big communities of more than a hundred. Unlike most other birds, eagles choose one mate for life.

🍽 Diet

Bald eagles are carnivores. Their preferred food is fish, but they'll eat other small animals such as rabbits, lizards, and smaller birds—living or dead! An eagle can also be a bit of a thief, stealing fish or other prey caught by other animals.

⚡ Dangers

PREDATORS: Adults: none; eggs: eaten by owls, raccoons, and squirrels

HUMAN CONFLICT: loss of habitat, climate change, environmental pollutants, hunting for sport or to protect livestock and fish

🔍 Exam Time

EXCELLENT EYES: When people say that someone is eagle-eyed, they mean that they're good at seeing detail. It's a good description—eagles have some of the best sight in the animal kingdom. Their eyes allow them to see both straight ahead and side to side at the same time, meaning they can see about three-quarters of the way around their heads!

HOLLOW BONES: Most birds that fly, including eagles, have pneumatic (new-MAT-tick), or hollow, bones. Eagles are very big, but they weigh very little. In fact, the entire skeleton of a bald eagle weighs less than half a pound (.23 kg), thanks to their hollow bones! This is one reason that eagles are so good at soaring high above the ground.

EXTRA TOE: Eagles have an extra toe, called a hallux. This fourth toe faces backward and helps an eagle keep hold of prey while in the air or during feeding.

SHARP BEAK: A sharp, barbed (hooked) beak sets raptors like eagles apart from other birds. Eagles use their beaks to tear into the flesh they eat.

WILD FACT!

A bald eagle isn't really bald. The word "bald" used to mean "white." The bald eagle got its name from the white feathers that cover its head. A baby bald eagle has brown feathers on its head, which are replaced with white ones as the eagle gets older.

GABBY SAYS!

One of the most common reasons I see eagles at the clinic is that they've run into problems with people. In the clinic, we may need to remove a wing to save a bird's life. When this happens, we don't release the bird back into the wild. Instead, it is given a spacious, protected home, and it is used to teach people about conservation.

153

GABBY SAYS!

A habitat becomes "fragmented" when human-made projects, such as roads and buildings, divide the area. This can be a real problem for animals like lynxes. Because they don't feel comfortable out in the open, they might not cross a newly created farmer's field, for example, even to find food or a mate. And that can lead to a drop in population.

CANADA LYNX

➕ Meet the Patient

Despite their name, Canada lynxes live not only in Canada, but also in parts of the United States, including Alaska. It's very hard to spot one in the wild. It's so hard, in fact, that some people call the lynx "the shadow of the forest."

🔍 Exam Time

TUFTED EARS: Furry tufts on the tips of a lynx's ears do more than help keep it warm. They also help gather more sound from the lynx's environment, so it can hear prey that is farther away.

LENGTHY BACK LEGS: Long back legs help a lynx leap over deep piles of snow.

SNOWSHOE-LIKE PAWS: Thick furry paws help spread out a lynx's weight over the snow. This keeps it from sinking into snowdrifts.

LYNX KITTENS

💜 Habitat and Family

These cats stay in the pine forest or on the rocky slopes of mountains. They are alone most of the time, although mother lynxes have been seen teaching their kittens how to hunt. Mother lynxes have between one and six kittens per year.

🍽 Diet

Canadian lynxes are carnivores. They mostly prey on snowshoe hares, but will eat other small animals if they find them.

⚡ Dangers

PREDATORS: adult: none; young: fishers (a type of weasel), birds of prey

HUMAN CONFLICT: hunting for fur; habitat loss, both for the lynxes and the hares they eat

THE VERY GOOD HELLBENDER

Even the animals that some people think are, well, less than beautiful get loving care when they come to my clinic. Just because an animal isn't fluffy doesn't mean that it lacks a cute personality.

Meet my friend the hellbender, for example—the largest amphibian in North America.

Once, more than 100 hellbenders at a zoo came down with a disease, and we had to dedicate an entire section of the clinic to their care. On top of that, each hellbender needed its own container so that it couldn't spread the disease!

We followed strict rules to make sure we took the very best care of these amphibians. We washed carefully, wore protective clothing, and tried very hard to keep the animals from getting stressed out.

Unfortunately, in addition to having the disease, some of the hellbenders had gotten into territorial fights and had scraped each other up. The losers of these fights often had a lot of open wounds, so we applied a gel to their skin to help soothe and heal it.

Later, we gave them a shot of medicine to help them heal faster. They all would squiggle and try to escape, except this one hellbender. Even though I had so many hellbenders to take care of, this one in particular became my little buddy. It seemed like he knew we were helping him. Either that, or he knew he was getting a treat for being a good hellbender!

When he saw me reaching in to give him his treatment for the day, he wouldn't run away—unlike all of the other animals. But what was even more surprising, he would tolerate the shot! You could tell he didn't like it, but he would be so good, patiently waiting while he got his medicine. I joked that maybe he had been through enough fights and sickness that he was saying, "Doc, this is nothing. I've literally been through everything!"

A HELLBENDER CAN SWALLOW A FISH ALMOST AS LONG AS ITS OWN BODY!

ALTHOUGH A HELLBENDER HAS LUNGS, IT BREATHES ALMOST ENTIRELY THROUGH ITS SKIN.

GABBY SAYS!

Being a wildlife vet means that I do a lot of work with babies. My friends at the Wolf Conservation Center in South Salem, New York, asked me to come out because of some exciting news: FOUR litters of wolves—two red wolf litters and two Mexican gray wolf litters. To help protect the puppies from disease, I needed to give them vaccines. Because the wolves live in a natural space full of places to hide, I got to go on a "wolf puppy treasure hunt" to try to find them all.

RED & MEXICAN WOLVES

➕ Meet the Patient

Is there any call of the wild more exciting than the howl of a wolf? North America is home to several species of wolves, including the critically endangered red and Mexican wolves.

🔍 Exam Time

RAIN-REPELLENT FUR: A wolf's coat has two layers: The undercoat, which grows close to the skin, helps keep the wolf warm, and the guard hairs, which grow on top of the undercoat, help to keep the undercoat dry.

AWESOME NOSE: A wolf's sense of smell is extremely keen. It is thought to be more than 100 times more powerful than a human's!

SCENT GLANDS: A wolf often leaves behind smells to communicate with other wolves. Special glands near its tail release scent messages that wolves use to identify each other, to mark territory, or just to say, "Leave me alone today!"

EXPRESSIVE BODIES: Like people, wolves use body language to communicate how they are feeling. A wolf with its neck, ears, and tail held high is likely showing interest in something. A lowered head and tail might mean fear or submission.

RED WOLF

MEXICAN WOLF

❤️ Habitat and Family

Most wolves live in packs that can have between 10 and 20 members. Packs are led by an alpha male and alpha female and include their offspring. Red wolves aren't as social as other wolves, and their packs usually only have 10 or so members. Both kinds of wolves have babies once a year, usually around three to six pups. Pups stay with the pack for a few years, until they strike out on their own.

🍽️ Diet

Wolves are carnivores. Though they will occasionally eat dead animals, they mostly prefer to hunt for their food, which includes deer, rabbits, fish, rodents, and other small animals.

⚡ Dangers

PREDATORS: adult: none; pups: birds of prey, lynxes, and bobcats

HUMAN CONFLICT: hunting and trapping to protect livestock, loss of habitat, diseases, including rabies and distemper, from domesticated dogs

WOLVES IN TLINGIT CULTURE

THE TLINGIT PEOPLE IDENTIFY AS ONE OF TWO CLANS: THE RAVEN CLAN AND THE WOLF OR EAGLE CLAN.

Living With Wolves

At one time, wolves ranged throughout most of what is now the United States and Canada. Many groups of Native Americans lived side by side with these mighty carnivores for thousands of years. It's no surprise, then, that the wolf plays a role in many of these peoples' traditions.

The Tlingit (thling-GIT) people are native to the Pacific Northwest regions of southeastern Alaska and Canada's British Columbia and Yukon territory. Several clans, or family groups, include the wolf as part of their crest. The animal is respected as a good hunter and defender of its family.

WOLVES ARE AN IMPORTANT PART OF THE PACIFIC NORTHWEST ECOSYSTEM.

Art

The Tlingit culture often honors the wolf in jewelry and other kinds of art. Tlingit artists sometimes carve totems, or symbols, out of cedar trees to help tell a story. If you understand the symbols, you can read the story, beginning at the top of the art and moving to the bottom.

CARVINGS OF A WOLF CAN SHOW THAT A CLAN, OR FAMILY, HAS ADOPTED THE WOLF AS A SYMBOL.

MUSIC AND DRUMS PLAY A LARGE ROLE IN TLINGIT CELEBRATIONS.

WOLVES ARE OFTEN PART OF TLINGIT STORIES AND ARE FOUND ON MANY PIECES OF TLINGIT ART.

Language

The Tlingit language is considered to be endangered because fewer and fewer people speak it as their everyday language. But just as people work to save endangered animals, people are working to save this language by teaching others about it!

LEARN SOME TLINGIT

THANK YOU	**gunalchéesh**
	(goon-alth-cheesh)
BALD EAGLE	**ch'aak'**
	(tch-AWK)
WOLF	**gooch**
	(gooch)

SEA & RIVER OTTERS

✚ Meet the Patient

North America is home to both river and sea otters. Quite social and playful, sea otters can be spotted in the Pacific Northwest, while river otters live throughout much of the eastern United States and Canada.

♥ Habitat and Family

A big group of sea otters is called a raft. Some rafts have more than 1,000 members! Groups of river otters are called lodges or bevys. Baby sea and river otters are called pups or kits. Sea otter pups aren't good divers when they're young—too much air gets trapped in their fur. That's a good thing. It gives them lots of time to practice swimming and diving. Before mother sea otters dive, they will sometimes wrap their pups in a piece of kelp to keep them from floating away.

🍽 Diet

Otters are carnivores. River otters eat fish and freshwater mussels; sea otters also eat fish, sea urchins, and other marine animals. Otters are super active, and need to eat a lot: They'll eat about a third of their body weight every day.

✎ Dangers

PREDATORS: orcas, great white sharks, eagles, coyotes, bears

HUMAN CONFLICT: habitat loss, pollution, hunting for fur and to protect fishing hauls

RIVER OTTERS

🔍 Exam Time

Unlike many other animals that live in the water, otters don't have a thick insulating layer of fat. Instead, they have two layers of hair—a guard layer and a softer undercoat. Air gets trapped between these two layers, keeping the otter toasty warm.

An otter's lungs are large. This allows the sea otter to dive deep and to stay underwater for up to five minutes. River otters can stay underwater for up to eight minutes.

Sea otters make good use of the time they spend underwater. If they catch more food than they can carry, they store it in pockets of extra skin and fur so they can keep swimming.

Sea otters float on their backs. River otters don't.

WILD FACT!

DOLPHINS & PORPOISES

There are more than 30 dolphin species and seven porpoise species in the world. Porpoises swim in waters close to the coasts of the North and South Poles, while dolphins swim in the warmer and deeper waters of the world's oceans.

VAQUITA, GULF OF CALIFORNIA

Vaquitas are porpoises that live only in the Gulf of California, a slim body of water off the coast of western Mexico. They are considered to be the most endangered of the whales, porpoises, and dolphins.

NORTH AMERICA

⚡ Dangers

These aquatic animals are under threat from more than pollution such as chemical spills or solid waste like plastic. They also face harm from loud sounds made by people. This noise can be harmful to these animals because they use their own system of sounds during echolocation. Human-made sounds disrupt the creatures' communication as well as their ability to hunt.

AMAZON RIVER DOLPHIN, BRAZIL

These dolphins live in the freshwaters of the Amazon River, and are the largest of the world's river dolphins. Adults can sometimes be almost pink in color!

SOUTH AMERICA

⚕ Health

During an exam, I give these mammals an "echolocation test." Echolocation begins when an animal makes a series of clicking noises. The noises move through the water until they bump into something (like a fish!). The sounds bounce off the object and travel back to the dolphin or porpoise. Both dolphins and porpoises have a structure in their head called a melon, which funnels the sounds to their brain. Then their brain uses this information to determine what's going on in the world around them!

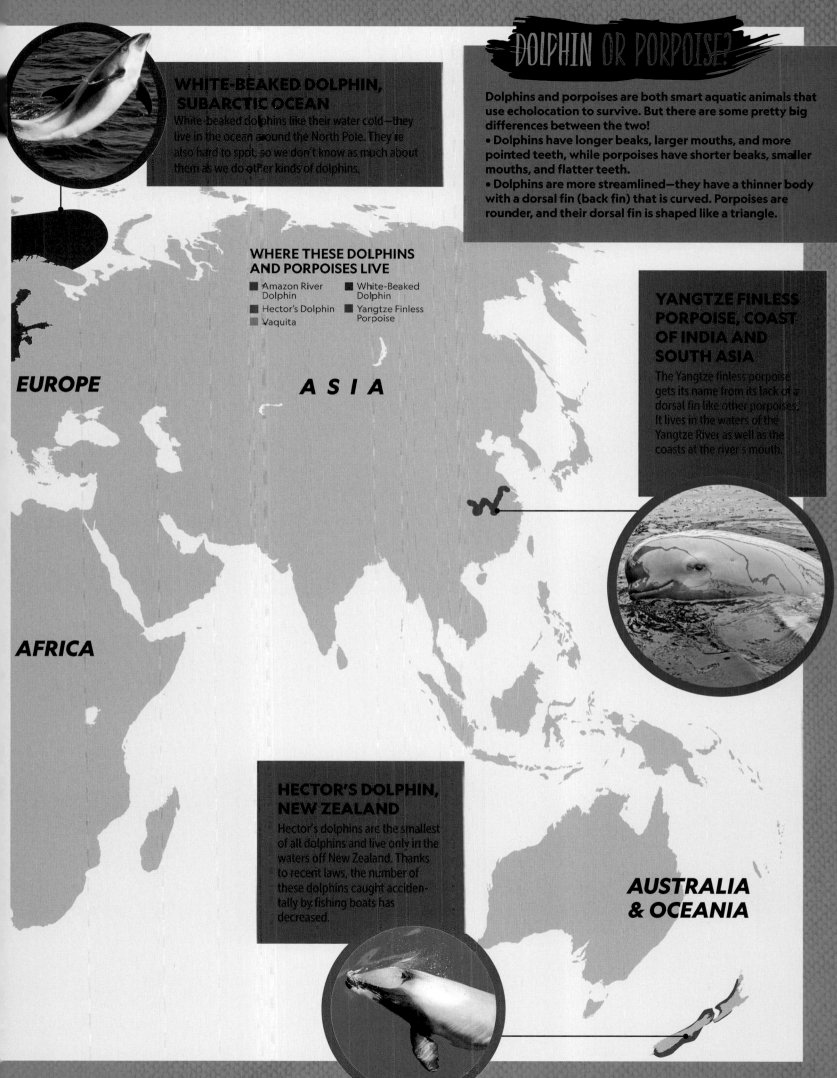

WHITE-BEAKED DOLPHIN, SUBARCTIC OCEAN

White-beaked dolphins like their water cold—they live in the ocean around the North Pole. They're also hard to spot, so we don't know as much about them as we do other kinds of dolphins.

DOLPHIN OR PORPOISE?

Dolphins and porpoises are both smart aquatic animals that use echolocation to survive. But there are some pretty big differences between the two!
• Dolphins have longer beaks, larger mouths, and more pointed teeth, while porpoises have shorter beaks, smaller mouths, and flatter teeth.
• Dolphins are more streamlined—they have a thinner body with a dorsal fin (back fin) that is curved. Porpoises are rounder, and their dorsal fin is shaped like a triangle.

WHERE THESE DOLPHINS AND PORPOISES LIVE

■ Amazon River Dolphin
■ Hector's Dolphin
■ Vaquita
■ White-Beaked Dolphin
■ Yangtze Finless Porpoise

EUROPE

ASIA

AFRICA

YANGTZE FINLESS PORPOISE, COAST OF INDIA AND SOUTH ASIA

The Yangtze finless porpoise gets its name from its lack of a dorsal fin like other porpoises. It lives in the waters of the Yangtze River as well as the coasts at the river's mouth.

HECTOR'S DOLPHIN, NEW ZEALAND

Hector's dolphins are the smallest of all dolphins and live only in the waters off New Zealand. Thanks to recent laws, the number of these dolphins caught accidentally by fishing boats has decreased.

AUSTRALIA & OCEANIA

GILA MONSTER

➕ Meet the Patient

This colorful creature is the largest native lizard in North America, living in the southwestern United States and northern Mexico. It gets its name from the Gila (HEE-lah) River, the place where it was discovered.

Gabby SAYS!

The Gila monster is the most venomous lizard in the United States. The lizard uses its venom mostly for self-defense, though. When it does bite, it hurts, so I do whatever it takes to avoid getting bitten!

♥ Habitat and Family

Gila monsters are hard to spot in the wild, so we don't know as much about their families as we know about some other kinds of reptiles. We do know that although they're not particularly social, Gila monsters can sometimes share shelter with one another even when it's not mating season. We also know that male lizards can be fierce fighters—they have wrestling matches to decide which lizard gets the best mate. And we know that female Gila monsters bury their eggs in a shallow hole in the ground, leaving them behind for the sun to keep warm. In a few months, the babies hatch and dig their way to the surface.

🍽 Diet

Gila monsters are carnivores and will eat whatever small animals they can catch and swallow whole, including reptiles, insects, amphibians, and birds. They are very fond of eggs and are often spotted climbing cacti looking for bird nests.

⚡ Dangers

PREDATORS: coyotes, birds of prey like hawks
HUMAN CONFLICT: habitat loss, killing by humans and pets, pet trade (taken as pets)

🔍 Exam Time

Gila monsters have to chew to push their venom into their "victims." The venom moves from their lower jaw through grooves in their teeth. Once a Gila monster bites, it doesn't let go very easily, either.

That tail is huge for a good reason: Gila monsters store fat in their tails, enough that they can go months without having a meal.

Gila monsters can't see very well, and they use their senses of smell and taste to find food. The lizard sticks out its tongue, "tasting" the air to sense prey nearby. A Gila monster can even track the trail made by a rolling egg!

WILD FACT! People used to think that the Gila monster's breath was toxic. Now we know that this isn't so. In fact, chemicals in the lizard's venom can be used to fight diseases in people.

WHITE-NOSED COATI

⊕ Meet the Patient

White-nosed coatis can be found in Mexico and parts of the southwestern United States. This tree-dwelling animal is about the size of a house cat, and is closely related to the raccoon.

♥ Habitat and Family

Coatis mostly live where there are plenty of trees, such as forests and rainforests. Some groups, though, will make their homes on grasslands or in the desert. Males prefer to be alone, but females travel in groups, called bands, of between 10 and 20 animals. Females leave the band to have their babies. They rejoin their band, along with their babies, when the babies are about six weeks old.

🍽 Diet

Coatis are omnivores and eat leaves, insects and spiders, and fruit. They'll eat other small animals, too, if they can catch them!

⚡ Dangers

PREDATORS: dogs, jaguars, large snakes, birds of prey

HUMAN CONFLICT: hunting for meat and fur, habitat loss

🔍 Exam Time

FLEXIBLE ANKLES: Coatis can walk down trees headfirst. That's because their ankles are flexible enough to turn backward.

SENSE OF SMELL: Coatis use scent to stay together as a group. Their keen sense of smell allows them to pick up on a scent that other coatis release from their neck and underbelly.

SHARP CLAWS: Coatis use their claws to defend themselves. But they also use them to dig up worms and other kinds of food from the ground.

LONG TAIL: A coatis uses its tail for balance as it climbs and as a "flag" for others to follow as it moves from tree to tree.

GABBY SAYS!

Whenever I need to gather up my coatis, it's easy! I just spray a scent they like—like a certain perfume—into the air, and they come running to me.

LOGGERHEAD TURTLE

+ Meet the Patient

Named after their large log-shaped heads, these reptiles are the world's largest hard-shelled turtle. They live in ocean waters around the world, including the coastal areas of the southern United States.

GABBY SAYS!

Working with turtles means meeting new challenges every day. Sometimes it means figuring out how to get an injured turtle to the rehabilitation center. Other times it means deciding how to treat a broken or cracked shell. And sometimes it means learning how to set up an aquarium that is best suited to helping an animal heal.

♥ Habitat and Family

Loggerhead turtles spend half their time in deep water and half in shallow water along the coast. Females come ashore to lay their eggs in a nest in the sand. Once the babies hatch, they wait until the temperature is cooler—this tells them it's night. Then they make their way into the ocean.

🍽 Diet

Loggerheads are omnivores. They eat just about anything, including sponges, sea stars, the eggs of other animals, and sea plants.

⚡ Dangers

PREDATORS: sharks, seals, orcas

HUMAN CONFLICT: bycatch (caught by fishermen); getting entangled in trash, discarded nets, other garbage; habitat loss; mistaking plastic bags for jellyfish and other food

WILD FACT! The temperature of the nest plays a role in whether a male or female baby loggerhead hatches from an egg. More females are born if the temperature is warm. More males are born if the temperature is cool.

🔍 Exam Time

STAY IN SHELL A turtle can't leave its shell. That's because some of its bones connect to the inside of it. The bottom of the shell, called the plastron, protects the turtle's belly. The top part, called the carapace, protects its back.

POWERED BY LUNGS Even though these turtles live in the ocean, they don't have gills. That means they need to breathe air at the water's surface. But because of their hard plastron, they can't flex their belly to take a breath. Instead, they use their leg muscles to move air in and out of their lungs.

POWERFUL JAWS Loggerheads pack a fierce bite. They need it to crack open the shells of the animals they eat, including crabs and conch.

COASTAL ENVIRONMENTS

Coastal environments form where the land meets the sea. These areas can take many forms, including rocky or sandy beaches, deltas and estuaries, wetlands, and rocky cliffs. Plants and animals living in these environments need to be hardy. With tides going in and out, plus the effects of wind and big and small waves, their habitat is constantly changing.

SOME ANIMALS THAT LIVE IN TIDE POOLS, SUCH AS THESE ANEMONES, ARE ABLE TO LIVE BOTH IN AND OUT OF THE WATER FOR SEVERAL HOURS AT A TIME.

RACCOONS AND OTHER SMALL ANIMALS CAN FIND PLENTY OF SHELLFISH, CRABS, AND OTHER PREY WHEN THE TIDE RECEDES.

BIG REPTILES LIKE CROCODILES AND ALLIGATORS OFTEN MAKE THEIR HOMES IN WETLANDS THAT FORM ALONG COASTS.

PEOPLE OFTEN VISIT TIDE POOLS TO WATCH WILDLIFE, LIKE THIS SEA LION. THIS PRESENTS A GREAT OPPORTUNITY FOR ME TO TEACH PEOPLE WHY THESE ECOSYSTEMS NEED TO BE CONSERVED.

🌿 Fast Facts

» Deltas and estuaries are areas where freshwater rivers meet the sea. Estuaries (the water areas) contain "brackish water," a mix of fresh- and salty water. Animals such as sea and river otters, clams, crabs, herons, and egrets make their home here.

» Every day, water advances onto shores with high tide, and then recedes with low tide, leaving pools of water behind. These pools are full of life that has adapted to an ever changing environment. Sea urchins, sea stars, and some kinds of octopuses can be found in tide pools.

🌱 Plant Life

Salty mangrove swamps, found in tropical and subtropical locations, are wetlands that get their name from a special tree called the mangrove. Unlike most trees, mangrove are able to live in salty water. Their roots also trap dirt, and it sometimes clumps together to form small areas of land. Mangrove swamps are home to lots of small animals like crabs, insects, and small birds. Larger animals, including monitor lizards, flying foxes, and crocodiles, come to the swamps in search of prey.

⭐ Good News

Where you find water, you'll usually find people. As a conservationist, part of my job is to teach people to be aware that they're sharing the sand and water with the wild plants and animals that live there.

I'VE MODELED IN FASHION PHOTOSHOOTS IN WHICH THE CLOTHES AND MAKEUP HAVE HELPED "TURN ME INTO" DIFFERENT ENDANGERED ANIMALS. HERE, I'M A FROG.

CONSERVATION:
ALWAYS IN STYLE

Fashion and conservation are often seen as a clash of two opposing worlds. Not only have animals historically been killed for their furs and skins, but the production of clothing has also created many problems, including water and air pollution, destruction of trees for factories, and other environmental damage that directly impacts animals. People are affected, too, especially those who are dependent on natural resources where they live.

We all wear clothes. And that means that we can all be part of the solution to this problem. We can try to wear clothing that is kind to the environment, to the people making the clothing, and to the animals.

For example, I now wear only sustainable and ethical fashion, from head to toe. Sustainable fashion has a small impact on the environment. For example, the dyes used don't cause water or air pollution. In ethical fashion, the process of clothing development—each stage of production from start to finish—is fair to the land, animals, and people involved.

As a wildlife veterinarian, it is my responsibility to make the lives of my patients better. And as an animal lover, changing my wardrobe to try to make a better and healthier planet was a "no-brainer."

MODELING MY *PROJECT RUNWAY* KAKAPO DRESS

In addition to being a wildlife vet, I'm an eco-fashion model. I work with designers around the world to model their clothes and spread the word about sustainable, ethical, responsible fashion. I've modeled in fashion shows that raise money for animal welfare.

I even spent one whole year wearing a different sustainably crafted outfit every month, each outfit representing a threatened animal. This experience was with the TV show *Project Runway*. The fashion designers, who had all competed on previous seasons of the show, were challenged to each create an outfit that represented an endangered animal. And there were some really creative results! The blue morpho butterfly dress was so pretty, and the kakapo parrot dress was like a rainbow of feathers. My favorite was the Bactrian camel—a super comfy tracksuit.

My eco-fashion modeling helps bring attention to endangered animals and build a sustainable clothing industry—as well as connect two things I love the most: I use any money I make from these projects to fund my foundation.

The Gabby Wild Foundation helps fund my travel to work with animals around the world. It also helps fund something very near and dear to my heart: rebuilding the Sumatran rainforest. This forest has been destroyed over time, resulting in the loss of homes for the animals that once lived here. Together with the Way Kambas National Park and local government, we're working to replant trees and bring back a thriving ecosystem.

There are so many ways to get involved and to do what you love. For me, wildlife veterinary work, fashion, and restoring habitats are my calling. And when I can do them all together, magic happens!

WANT TO BE A VET?

You'll find a veterinarian anywhere you find animals. Different kinds of vets specialize, or choose to work with different animals in different places.

I mostly work with wildlife, but other vets work only with peoples' pets. A veterinarian might, for example, work in a zoo, or strictly with animals that live in the ocean. Other vets tend to farm animals, or might only work with birds or reptiles. The important thing is to be able to work with both the animals and also people, especially in situations that are a little bit stressful.

And there are other jobs vets can do, too. Some veterinarians act as private detectives, looking for lost pets. Other vets work to find cures or new vaccines for animal diseases. And some even teach students to become the next generation of vets!

IF YOU LIKE TO ...	THEN YOU MIGHT ...
... work with dogs and cats	... become a **SMALL ANIMAL VET!** These vets work in an animal hospital, doing checkups on people's pets.
... work with birds, rabbits, and reptiles	... become a **POCKET EXOTIC ANIMAL VET!** Exotic pet vets work with other small ("pocket") animals that people keep as pets.
... work with horses	... become an **EQUINE VET!** Equine vets visit farms and stables, checking on racehorses, farm horses, and pet horses.
... work with farm animals	... specialize in **FARM ANIMAL MEDICINE!** These vets spend a lot of time outside visiting farms to check on cows, pigs, sheep, and chickens.

Being a vet is a lot of hard work *and* a lot of fun! If you think that it's the right path for you, here are some things you can do right now.

STUDY SCIENCE.
Life science (biology) is super important, but if you like chemistry or environmental science, those are good places to start, too!

READ. One of the best things you can do is to learn all you can about animals. Take a trip to the library, hit a bookstore, or surf the web (with an adult's permission). Just read as much as you can!

VISIT A ZOO OR A MUSEUM.
If you have a chance to visit a zoo or museum, take it. Can't make the trip? With an adult's permission, try a virtual zoo at the World Association of Zoos and Aquariums site: www.waza.org.

GO WITH YOUR PET TO THE VET. If your dog or cat is due for a vet visit, go along. It will give you a good idea about what vets do during an exam. Plus, it's a great opportunity to ask questions.

LEARN MORE!

Want to learn even more about how to become an animal doctor? Check out the info below!

VISIT (with an adult's permission)
- www.careergirls.org/career/veterinarian
- www.cbc.ca/kidscbc2/the-feed/so-you-want-to-be-a-vet
- kids.nationalgeographic.com/videos/awesome-animal-vets (videos of Nat Geo vets working with animals and talking about being a vet and how to be a good pet owner)
- kids.nationalgeographic.com/explore/adventure_pass/amazing-animals (more animal rescue stories)

MEET THE NAT GEO WILD VETS:
- Dr. Pol: www.nationalgeographic.com/tv/shows/the-incredible-dr-pol
- Dr. Oakley: www.natgeotv.com/ca/dr-oakley-yukon-vet
- Dr. K: http://natgeotv.com/ca/dr-ks-exotic-animal-er

READ
- National Geographic Kids Chapters series for more animal fun, rescues, and heroes, available wherever books are sold
- National Geographic Kids Mission: Animal Rescue series for more about saving endangered animals

WANT TO GET INVOLVED?

NORTH AMERICA

EUROPE

AFRICA

SOUTH AMERICA

Humans live in almost 200 countries around the world. Animals, though, don't care where a country begins and ends, or which part of the ocean is part of what country. For example, this map shows where we can find loggerhead turtles. As you can see, these creatures can be found all over the world. Their habitat spans the entire globe.

What can people learn from this? We all have a part to play in helping to save animals. We all matter. And by working together, we can make a big difference.

WHERE LOGGERHEAD TURTLES LIVE

■ Loggerhead Turtle

ASIA

AUSTRALIA & OCEANIA

With an adult, check out the work of these worldwide organizations:

Africa

AFRICAN WILDLIFE FOUNDATION: The AWF works with leaders of African governments to promote conservation of its countries' lands and animals. This organization considers the needs of both animals and people, and promotes the idea that protecting Africa's wildlife is an essential part of Africa's future.
www.awf.org

JANE GOODALL INSTITUTE: The Jane Goodall Institute promotes the conservation of chimpanzees and other great apes by combining education, empowerment, and science. The institute believes that the understanding of how people and animals are connected makes the planet better for everyone.
www.janegoodall.org

Asia

SUMATRAN ORANGUTAN CONSERVATION PROGRAMME: The SOCP protects orangutans and their habitat. Its primary goal is increasing the number of these animals in the wild. It works toward this goal through the successful reintroduction of illegally captured animals and protection of orangutan habitat.
www.sumatranorangutan.org

Europe

ZOOLOGICAL SOCIETY OF LONDON EDGE OF EXISTENCE PROGRAMME: This program focuses on protecting species that are Evolutionarily Distinct (ED) and Globally Endangered (GE). EDGE animals are not as well-known as many endangered species; they have few (if any) close relatives on Earth, and are essential in keeping the planet's biodiversity strong.
www.edgeofexistence.org

North America

WOLF CONSERVATION CENTER: The WCC works to protect and preserve wolves in North America. The center hopes to accomplish this goal through education and by participating in the recovery and release programs for red and Mexican gray wolves.
www.nywolf.org

LOGGERHEAD MARINELIFE CENTER: The LMC serves as both a wildlife hospital and a conservation center that works to improve ocean ecosystems and the endangered turtles that live in them.
www.marinelife.org

Oceania

KAKAPO RECOVERY: New Zealand's Department of Conservation works with educators, volunteers, and scientists to help the number of this critically endangered bird to increase.
www.doc.govt.nz/our-work/kakapo-recovery

Central America

BELIZE ZOO AND TROPICAL EDUCATION CENTER: This zoo and education center believes that educational programs about the land and its animals will inspire people to take positive steps toward conservation.
www.belizezoo.org

Global

WILDLIFE CONSERVATION SOCIETY: The WCS's mission is to save wildlife and preserve wild lands by combining research, education, public action, and inspiration.
www.wcs.org

INTERNATIONAL UNION FOR CONSERVATION OF NATURE: The goal of the IUCN is to help people all over the world to conserve nature and to use natural resources wisely. It is considered the authority on the world's endangered species.
www.iucn.org

WHAT SHOULD YOU DO IF YOU FIND AN ANIMAL?

You're out for a walk, or hike ... or maybe you're just playing in your neighborhood or backyard, and you come across an animal that looks like it needs help. What should you do?

1. DON'T TOUCH IT. The animal might be hurt or sick, and almost definitely will be scared. It might try to bite or scratch you, even if you are trying to help it.

2. TELL AN ADULT. Together, call your local humane society or city wildlife manager. They can help you know what next steps to take and what resources are available in your area.

3. DON'T KEEP IT. It's never a good idea to keep wildlife as a pet. Even if the animal seems to be tame, it is still a wild animal!

GLOSSARY

Here are some helpful wildlife words.

adaptation a behavior or body part an animal has that helps it survive in its environment

alpha the animal in a group that is in charge or has the most power

arachnid the group of animals that includes spiders, ticks, and scorpions

archipelago (ar-kih-PELL-ih-go) a large group of islands

biodiversity the collection of different kinds of living things in an area

biome (BY-ohm) an area of the world that has the same climate and kinds of plants

browser an animal that eats parts of plants that grow high above the ground, like twigs, shoots, and leaves

carnivore an animal that eats mostly meat

climate the weather conditions in an area over a long period of time

cold-blooded describes an animal that has a body temperature that changes as the temperature of its environment changes

conservation the protection and careful use of things in nature

deforestation the cutting down, burning, or otherwise removal of trees in an area

delta a triangle-shaped land area at the mouth of a river

domesticated (duh-MESS-tih-kated) describes an animal that is tame or used to living and working with humans

echolocation (ek-oh-low-KAY-shun) the ability of some animals to locate prey or other objects by bouncing soundwaves off them

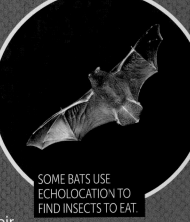
SOME BATS USE ECHOLOCATION TO FIND INSECTS TO EAT.

ecology (ee-CALL-uh-jee) the study of living things in their environment

ecosystem all of the living and non-living things in an area

endangered describes any kind of living thing that is in danger of disappearing from Earth

estuary a water environment where a river meets the sea

extinct describes any kind of living thing that once lived on Earth, but does not anymore

SNAKES AND OTHER REPTILES ARE COLD-BLOODED.

KANGAROOS ARE PROBABLY AUSTRALIA'S MOST FAMOUS MARSUPIAL.

habitat   the place where an animal lives

herbivore (HERB-ih-vore)   an animal that eats mostly plants

marsupial (mar-SOUP-ee-al)   any of a group of mammals, such as a koala or kangaroo, that are born very small and finish developing in pouches

monotreme (MON-oh-treem)   a group of mammals, including platypuses and echidnas, that are hatched from eggs

nocturnal (nock-TURN-al)   active or mostly active at night

omnivore (OM-nih-vore)   an animal that eats both plants and meat

poaching   illegal hunting or illegally taking an animal from its habitat

pollinator   an animal that helps plants reproduce by carrying pollen

predator   an animal that hunts and eats other animals

prey   an animal that is hunted and eaten by other animals

solitary (SOLL-ih-tare-ee)   describes animals that live alone, usually only coming together to mate

species (SPEE-sheez)   a particular kind of animal

threatened   describes an animal that is likely to become endangered unless something changes

venom   a toxin injected into another animal through a bite or sting

vulnerable   describes an animal that has the possibility of becoming endangered because of habitat loss

CHEETAHS ARE AN ENDANGERED SPECIES.

warm-blooded   describes an animal that uses energy to keep its body temperature steady at all times

HEDGEHOGS ARE OMNIVORES, AND WILL EAT BOTH PLANTS AND SMALL ANIMALS.

VETERINARY
GLOSSARY

Here are some helpful words for veterinarians-in-training.

anesthesia (annn-ess-THEE-yah) a gas or drug given to an animal to make it sleepy or keep it from feeling pain

binocular vision the type of seeing that occurs when both eyes view the same thing at once

bladder a small organ in the body that holds urine (pee) until it leaves the body

carapace (KAIR-uh-pace) the top part of a turtle's or tortoise's shell

cartilage (CART-ih-lidj) the bendable tissue that is part of an animal's skeleton, such as at the end of your nose

chytrid (KY-trid) a kind of fungus that causes a disease in amphibians

cloven (CLOVE-en) split into two parts

distemper (diss-TEM-purr) a disease in cats and dogs that causes fever and coughing

feral (FER-al) describes an animal that is usually tame, such as a dog or a cat, that lives wild instead

guard hair a long, thick hair that forms the outer layer of fur on some animals

history a list of facts about an animal's past health

imprinting an animal's learning how to act from another animal and becoming attached to it, usually to one of its parents

incisor (in-SIGH-zor) a tooth near the front of an animal's mouth usually used to bite

keratin (CARE-uh-tin) a tough, waterproof material found in claws, nails, feathers, and horns

knuckle the place in a finger or toe where two bones meet and form a joint that can bend

A CAMEL'S FOOT IS CLOVEN.

THIS GALÁPAGOS TORTOISE'S CARAPACE AND PLASTRON FORM THE TOP AND BOTTOM OF ITS SHELL.

larva a recently hatched wormlike baby insect; plural: larvae (LARV-ee)

membrane a thin sheet of tissue in a living thing

papillae (pap-PILL-ee) a bump that helps an animal to taste, touch, or smell

pheromone (FARE-uh-mone) a chemical that can change the behavior of another animal of the same species

plastron (PLAST-run) the bottom (underside) of a turtle or tortoise shell

GILA MONSTERS ARE VENOMOUS REPTILES.

pneumatic (new-MAT-tick) bone a bone that is hollow

prehensile (pre-HENS-ul) describes a tail or lip that is able to wrap around and grasp objects like branches or food

rabies (RAY-bees) a brain disease caused by a virus that is passed from mammal to mammal

regenerate (ree-JEN-ur-ate) to be able to grow back, like a leg or tentacle

signalment (SIG-nall-ment) the basic facts about an animal, such as its species, its age, and its sex

tapetum (tuh-PEE-tum) a part of the back of the eye that can reflect light

venom a toxin injected into another animal through a bite or sting

vomit to throw up

virus a very small germm that can cause disease

zoonotic (zoh-uh-NOT-tick) describes a disease that can be passed back and forth between animals and people

INDEX

Boldface indicates illustrations.

INDEX

CREDITS

COVER

(BACKGROUND), alwaysloved afilm/SS; (UP RT), Becky Hale/NG Staff; (LO RT), NightOwlZA/GI; (CTR), Mikadun/SS; (LO LE), Matthijs Kuijper/Alamy Stock Photo; (CTR LE), mgkuijpers/Adobe Stock; (UP LE), buteo/Adobe Stock; back cover (BACKGROUND), Tashile/SS; (UP), Gabby Wild; (CTR), Lillian King/GI; (LO), pixelfreund/Adobe Stock; spine, Mikadun/SS

FRONT MATTER

1 (texture throughout), alwaysloved afilm/SS; 1 (pattern throughout), Tashi/SS; 1, Becky Hale/NGP Staff; 2 (UP LE), NGIC; 2 (UP RT), gmlykin/SS; 2 (CTR), Jenner Images/GI; 2 (LO RT), NGIC; 2 (LO LE), NGIC; 3 (UP RT), Frans Lanting/NGIC; 3 (LO RT), Oksana Schmidt/GI; 3 (CTR), Dr. Gabby Wild; 3 (LO LE), Csaba Esvég/EyeEm/GI; 3 (UP LE), Fred Bavendam/MP/NGIC; 4 (UP), Konrad Wothe/MP; 4 (LO), Artush/SS; 5 (UP LE), Willi Rolfes/BIA/MP; 5 (UP RT), GI/iStockphoto; 5 (CTR), Winfried Wisniewski/MP/NGIC; 5 (LO), markuskessler/GI/iStockphoto; 6 (paper), Stephen Rees/SS; 6 (LO LE), j.wootthisak/SS; 7 (UP), Dr. Gabby Wild; 7 (LO RT), Konrad Wothe/MP; 7 (LO LE), Danita Delmont/Alamy Stock Photo; 8-9, Dr. Gabby Wild; 8 (dog), Mila Atkovska/SS; 8 (snow leopard), Nagel Photography/SS

SOUTH & CENTRAL AMERICA

11, Dr. Gabby Wild; 12-13, Tom Walker/GI; 12 (UP), Todamo/SS; 12 (LO), Ondrej Prosicky/SS; 13 (LO), Becky Hale/NGP Staff; 14-15, gmlykin/SS; 14 (LO), Tui De Roy/MP/NGIC; 15 (UP), Tui De Roy/MP; 15 (LO), Becky Hale/NGP Staff; 16-17, Jess Kraft/SS; 17 (UP), Uwe Bergwitz/SS; 17 (LO), Gudkov Andrey/SS; 18-19, Lonely Planet Images/GI; 18 (LO), Becky Hale/NGP Staff; 19 (UP), Mary Ann McDonald/GI; 19 (LO), Steve Meese/SS; 20-21, Janusz Pienkowski/SS; 20 (UP), Nicole Duplaix/NGIC; 21 (UP), Artush/SS; 21 (LO), Becky Hale/NGP Staff; 22-23, Juergen & Christine Sohns/GI; 22 (LO), Becky Hale/NGP Staff; 23 (UP), Milan Zygmunt/SS; 23 (LO), Oliver Lambert/GI; 24 (UP LE), Tom McHugh/Science Source; 24 (UP RT), imageBROKER/Alamy Stock Photo; 24 (LO), Dirk Ercken/SS; 25 (UP), Best View Stock/Alamy Stock Photo; 25 (CTR), Lenorko/SS; 25 (LO), Hurly D'souza/SS; 26-27, Doug Schnurr/Alamy Stock Photo; 26 (LE), Charly Morlock/SS; 26 (RT), Eric Isselee/SS; 27 (LO), Becky Hale/NGP Staff; 28, Luciano Candisani/MP; 28 (LO), Becky Hale/NGP Staff; 29 (UP), Klein and Hubert/MP; 29 (CTR), Steve Winter/NGIC; 29 (LO), ZSSD/MP; 30-31, Dr. Gabby Wild; 31 (UP), iStockphoto/GI; 32-33, Christian Ziegler/NGIC; 32, Visuals Unlimited/GI; 33 (LO), Rebecca Hale/National Geographic Images; 34-35, OCollins/SS; 35 (UP), Iakov Filimonov/SS; 35 (LO), Stefano Buttafoco/SS; 35 (LO LE), Becky Hale/NGP Staff; 36 (UP), Cinematographer/SS; 36 (LO), MP cz/SS; 37 (UP), Danita Delimont/

Alamy Stock Photo; 37 (CTR), Robert and Lisa Sainsbury Collection/Bridgeman Images; 37 (RT), Allen.G/SS

EUROPE

39, Dr. Gabby Wild; 40-41, Norayr Avagyan/GI; 40 (LO), Becky Hale/NGP Staff; 41 (UP), Philartphace/GI; 41 (LO), Ondrej Prosicky/SS; 42-43, Dr. Gabby Wild; 44-45, Marco Pozzi/GI; 44 (LE), Fotofeeling/GI; 44 (RT), Joanne Hedger/GI; 45 (LO), Becky Hale/NGP Staff; 46, Michael Quinton/MP; 47 (UP), Visuals Unlimited, Inc./Patrick Endres/GI; 47 (CTR), Ingo Arndt/MP; 47 (LO), Sergio Pitamitz/NGIC; 48-49, Konrad Wothe/MP; 49 (UP), Oscar Diez/BIA/MP; 49 (CTR), Federica Grassi/GI; 49 (LO), Becky Hale/NGP Staff; 50-51, Willi Rolfes/BIA/MP; 50 (LO), Lillian King/GI; 51 (LO), Becky Hale/NGP Staff; 52 (UP LE), Georgi Baird/SS; 52 (UP RT), niaonet.com Bird Photography/GI; 52 (LO RT), JMx Images/SS; 52 (LO LE), Kjersti Joergensen/SS; 53 (LO LE), Arco Images GmbH/Alamy Stock Photo; 53 (LO RT), Auscape/UIG/GI; 54-55, AttilaBarsan/GI54 (LO), Becky Hale/NGP Staff; 55 (UP), Stockphoto/GI; 55 (LO), Nature Photographers Ltd/Alamy Stock Photo; 56, Moment RF/GI; 57 (UP), Elliotte Rusty Harold/SS; 57 (LO), Konrad Wothe/NPL/MP; 58-59, Erika Carrera/EyeEm/GI; 58 (LO), BarbAnna/GI; 59 (LO), Becky Hale/NGP Staff; 60, Alamy Ltd, 127 Milton Park; 61 (UP), Kike Calvo/NGIC; 61 (LO), BlackDorianstock/SS

AFRICA

63, Dr. Gabby Wild; 64-65, Joel Sartore/NGIC; 65 (UP), Johan Swanepoel/SS; 65 (LO), prapass/SS; 66-67, Nigel Pavitt/GI; 66 (UP), Nigel Pavitt/GI; 66 (LO), Four Oaks/SS; 67 (LO), Becky Hale/NGP Staff; 68 (UP), Tony Barnett; 68 (LO), Winfried Wisniewski/MP/NGIC: 69 (UP), Gudkov Andrey/SS; 69 (CTR), Tony Barnett; 69 (LO), Ondrej Prosicky/SS; 70, Barbara Von Hoffmann/NGIC; 71 (RT), Barrie Britton/Nature Picture Library; 71 (LE), Petr Simon/SS; 71 (LO), Becky Hale/NGP Staff; 72, Mark Pearson/Alamy Stock Photo; 73 (UP), Dr. Gabby Wild; 73 (LO), Petr Simon/SS; 74-75, Ronan Donovan/NGIC; 75 (UP), Henri Bouyat/500px/GI; 75 (LO), Becky Hale/NGP Staff; 76, Robert Harding Picture Library/NGIC; 77 (UP), Suzi Eszterhas/MP; 77 (CTR), Michael Poliza/NGIC; 77 (LO), Mary Ann McDonald/SS; 78, Paul Souders/GI; 78 (LO), Becky Hale/NGP Staff; 79 (UP), Michael Melford/NGIC; 79 (LO), Christian Musat/SS; 80-81, Nigel Pavitt/GI; 81 (UP), Pete Oxford/MP; 81 (CTR), Eric Isselee/SS; 81 (LO), Becky Hale/NGP Staff; 82 (UP RT), Colin Langford/GI; 82 (LO RT), Roland Seitre/MP; 82 (LO LE), Roland Seitre/MP; 82 (UP LE), moosehenderson/SS; 83 (UP), Ernie Janes/NPL/MP; 83 (LO), Gudkov Andrey/SS; 84-85, beataaldridge/Adobe Stock; 84 (UP), Patrick Kientz/Biosphoto/MP; 84 (LO), Anup Shah/MP; 85 (LO), Becky Hale/NGP Staff; 86-86 (LO), Becky Hale/NGP Staff; 87, Joel Sartore/NGIC; 87, cynoclub/iStockphoto/GI; 88 (UP), Cyril Ruoso/MP/NGIC; 88 (LO), Ingo Arndt/MP/NGIC; 89 (UP), Jason Edwards/NGIC; 89 (LO), Becky Hale/NGP Staff; 90-91, Dr. Gabby